“So you’re ... interested?”

Dylan leaned in deliberately, watching Maxine’s eyes. They were the color of topaz, streaked with green near the pupils, a green that disappeared as they darkened. They might also have been damning him to hell, but they darkened. He could hear her breathing speed up. “It’s dangerous to twist the tail of a tiger,” he murmured. “You never know what’ll happen.”

And then he felt it, a tremor running through her, faint as the flap of butterfly wings.

Need punched through him, taking him by surprise. Suddenly, what had started out as a test of wills had turned into something quite different. Suddenly, he was testing himself—and coming up wanting. Dylan Reynolds was a man used to being in control of his desires, but for a disconcerting moment, he wasn’t anymore. He could feel each breath as she exhaled, knew how little it would take to bridge the gap between them. Just one taste, he bargained with himself, ignoring the knowledge that one taste would only lead to the next. Just one, he promised, lowering his lips toward hers.

Dear Reader,

The minute Max walked on stage in *The Chef's Choice,* I knew she had to have a book of her own. A woman like Max couldn't be matched up with just any guy, though, so Stephen and I went hunting in our heads and unearthed a sexy, charming architect who's just a little too cocky for his own good. All I had to do then was set them at odds with each other and bring their world alive while I let them battle it out. One of the best things about this job is the marvelous places the job takes me. To write Max and Dylan's story, I not only had to visit the remarkably cool city of Portland several times (I was forced, I tell you), but I found myself traveling over the Internet to places like Dubai. I hope you enjoy the results and find yourself smiling along the way.

I'd love to hear what you think of Max and Dylan, so drop me a line at kristin@kristinhardy.com. And don't forget to watch for the stories of Walker and Tucker—and maybe even Glory, if I can talk my editor into it. In the meantime, stop by www.kristinhardy.com for news, recipes and contests. Don't forget to sign up for my newsletter to be informed of new releases.

Enjoy!

Kristin Hardy

THE BOSS'S PROPOSAL

KRISTIN HARDY

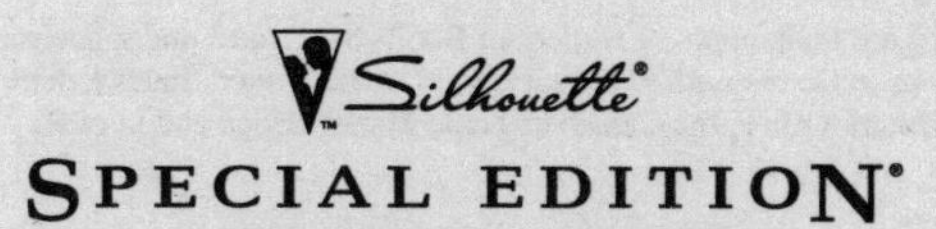

Published by Silhouette Books
America's Publisher of Contemporary Romance

Recycling programs for this product may not exist in your area.

ISBN-13: 978-0-373-65540-3

THE BOSS'S PROPOSAL

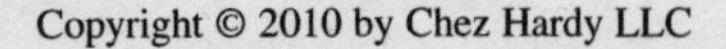

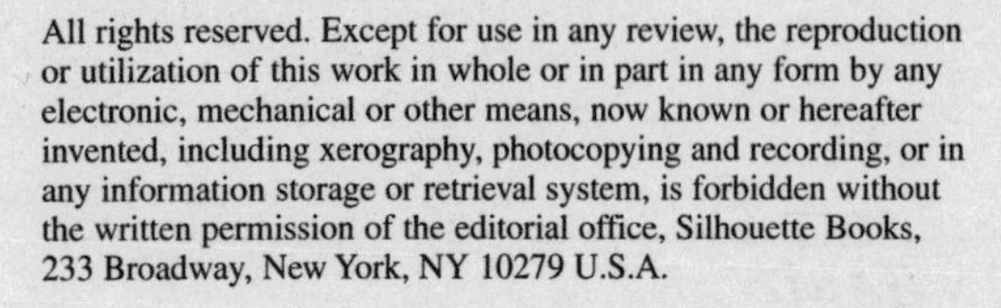

This edition published by arrangement with Harlequin Books S.A.

For questions and comments about the quality of this book please contact us at Customer_eCare@Harlequin.ca.

Visit Silhouette Books at www.eHarlequin.com

Printed in U.S.A.

Books by Kristin Hardy

Silhouette Special Edition

††*Where There's Smoke* #1720
††*Under the Mistletoe* #1725
††*Vermont Valentine* #1739
††*Under His Spell* #1786
***Always a Bridesmaid* #1832
Her Christmas Surprise #1871
‡‡*The Chef's Choice* #1919
††*Always Valentine's Day* #1952
~*A Fortune Wedding* #1976
‡‡*The Boss's Proposal* #2058

Harlequin Blaze

My Sexiest Mistake #44
**Scoring* #78
**As Bad As Can Be* #86
**Slippery When Wet* #94
†*Turn Me On* #148
†*Cutting Loose* #156
†*Nothing but the Best* #164
§*Certified Male* #187
§*U.S. Male* #199
Caught #242
Bad Influence #295
Hot Moves #307
Bad Behavior #319

††Holiday Hearts
**Logan's Legacy Revisited
‡‡The McBains of Grace Harbor
*Under the Covers
†Sex & the Supper Club
§Sealed with a Kiss
~Fortunes of Texas: Return to Red Rock

KRISTIN HARDY

has always wanted to write, starting her first novel while still in grade school. Although she became a laser engineer by training, she never gave up her dream of being an author. In 2002, her first completed manuscript, *My Sexiest Mistake,* debuted in Harlequin's Blaze line; it was subsequently made into a movie by the Oxygen network. Kristin lives in New Hampshire with her husband and collaborator. Check out her Web site at www.kristinhardy.com.

To Gail "the Goddess" Chasan,
for more than I can possibly say,
to Shannon, Sylvie, and Teresa,
because it took a village to raise this baby,
and to Stephen,
because it only takes one man…
as long as he's the right one.

Acknowledgments

Thanks go to
Angie Knutson-Smith, AIA, LEED AP, of Altus Studios,
former Bergman Associates whip-cracker Shannon Short,
and Susan Hardy, RN, of the
St. Joseph Hospital Oncology Center
for helping me bring the process alive

Chapter One

"Boiled or fried?" Maxine McBain glanced at her friend Glory Bishop.

"The shrimp?" Glory paused in the process of biting into an appetizer from the gala's buffet line.

"Jeremy Simmons."

Glory frowned. "Max, what are you talking about?"

"I'm trying to decide what to do with my illustrious project manager when he gets here. *If* he gets here."

Glory shook her head. "And people tell me I'm nuts."

"You're right. Boiling or frying is way too much trouble."

"Good, because I—"

"I'll just throw him on the barbecue instead."

Glory opened her mouth and closed it again. "Not worried about the life in prison part, I take it?"

"There's not a jury in the country who would convict me," Max said serenely, taking a sip of her club soda. "The fundraiser's been going on for over an hour. No Jeremy, no phone call, no text, no nothing. Unless he's hospitalized or stranded in Tierra del Fuego, he's going to have to do some fast talking."

"Tierra del Fuego?"

"Possibly Outer Mongolia. Somewhere far from here."

They stood at one of the tables of the silent auction near a trio of Glory's metal sculptures. Around them rose the buzz of conversation from several hundred people, punctuated by bursts of laughter. White-jacketed servers circulated beneath the light of glittering chandeliers, offering canapés and champagne. Over in the corner, the singer for the cover band did his best to sound like John Fogerty as he sang about big wheels turning.

Well, they knew their audience, all right, Max thought. Dressed in silks and satins and tuxedos were gathered the biggest wheels of Maine, including the wealthy summer people from Kennebunkport to Castine. If all went well, those deep-pocket donors would fund the construction of Portland General Medical Center's new oncology wing. And if all really went well, Portland General would hire Becker, Reynolds and Stein, Max's employer, to design it.

Max set her empty glass on the tray of a passing waiter, giving him a smile brilliant enough to have him looking back over his shoulder as he walked away. Max didn't pay much attention—she had other things on her mind. "All right, that's it, we go to plan B," she said to Glory briskly. "Come on."

"Come on where?"

"To schmooze the medical center brass."

"Weren't you the one telling me your boss expressly forbid you to talk to the Portland General people without him?"

Max adjusted one of her gold bracelets. "Jeremy only thinks he's my boss. I report to Hal Reynolds. Jeremy's just the head of the proposal team."

"So why isn't Reynolds here to schmooze the brass if this project's so important? Or one of the other partners?"

"Hal's in Munich at a conference. Leo Stein's at his daughter's wedding in L.A. John Becker retired last year…to Boca Raton, I think. That makes us the only ones here. And the only ones available to bond."

"I've got a better idea. You bond, and I'll eat. There are these little chocolate-covered thingies that look— Hey," Glory complained as Max neatly plucked the martini glass from her hand and set it aside. "I needed that."

"We bond," Max said firmly. "You're supposed to be starving for your art, remember?"

They'd met three years before at the gallery where Glory was holding her first show. In the time since, Glory's professional star had risen, due in no small part to the exposure she'd gotten from placing sculptures at several BRS projects. She and Max had become fast friends, the dark, compact, unconventional Glory providing the perfect foil for Max's warm blond looks. They shared a love of fiery hot ethnic food, cool jazz and bad horror films, the dumber the better.

"But I'm tired of being a starving artist," Glory protested, eyeing the dessert table. "I want to be a reasonably well-fed yet still enviably thin artist. Besides, I'm just supposed to do the art for the medical center's sculpture garden. You're the genius who's on the hook to design the place."

"We have to get the project first. And who was the one going on about the price of acetylene last week?" Max shook her shoulder-length hair back and smoothed down her dress. "You need the job as much as I do, Bishop, so come on."

"But I'm not dressed to win projects," Glory tried, tugging at the marigold-colored broomstick skirt she'd paired with a purple camisole.

"You're not in your overalls and a welding helmet, are you?" Max asked, glancing at Glory's outfit. "You'll wake them up. Besides, you're the temperamental artist, you can wear whatever you want and they'll just think you're being colorful."

Max had spent far more time than she cared to admit picking out her dress for the evening. There was always a fine line to tread at these sorts of events: too glitzy and they didn't take you seriously, too dowdy and you stuck out more than if you'd overdressed. She'd settled on a sleeveless sheath, beautifully cut but utterly simple. Her sole concession to vanity was the fabric, a deep bronze silk that whispered against her skin.

"Now you're getting bossy," Glory muttered. "Deep down, you just want the project so you can push everybody around."

"I don't push people around. I just help them realize what's best for them."

"Funny how what's best for them tends to be what you want."

Max grinned. "I'm naturally intuitive that way. And besides, I—" She broke off as her cell phone vibrated. "About time," she muttered as she fished it out of her evening bag.

"Give Jeremy my love," Glory said and strode purposefully toward the array of desserts.

Max glanced at the display and blinked, her brow creasing, before she flipped it open. "Hal? What… Where are you?" And what was he doing calling her when he was supposed to be flying home?

"I'm in D.C., making my connection. We just landed."

"Oh." To get some privacy, she moved away from the tables toward the entrance. "How was Munich?"

"Fine. At least what I saw of it. Arianne liked it. Listen, I got a call from Jeremy Simmons before I took off."

Her uneasiness crystallized. "What's going on? He's not here."

"And he won't be. He's jumped ship to a London firm that's working on one of the Olympic venues."

"You're kidding." Max stared. "*Jeremy* gave you notice over the phone?"

"He didn't give me notice. He told me he was on his way out the door. Apparently they want him in London on Monday."

Max glanced at the medical center board members across the room. "He always said living here was turning him into a savage. So where does that leave the firm?" And where did it leave her?

"Long term we'll be fine. I've got to talk to Leo, though. Jeremy left a lot of balls in the air—like the one you're hanging on to right now. I know the deadline on the Portland General project is coming up. We'll get you some help right away."

"Hal, don't worry about it. I can take care of things—in all honesty, I've been doing all the legwork and preliminary design already, anyway." And after six years of school and seven years at the firm, she was tired of getting the job done by coming up with a good idea and then convincing whoever she was reporting to that they'd thought of it themselves. After seven years of paying her dues, she was ready to be the boss.

"Look, Max, both Leo and I are aware of how much you've been doing, but this project is our ticket into the health care design market. We need someone with a track record."

"Give me a chance, Hal." Her words were low and intense. "I can do this."

He hesitated and she could hear her heart beat in the silence. "Look, we don't have to solve this now," he said finally. "For tonight, wave the flag with the medical center folks and keep the news about Jeremy to yourself. We'll talk about the proposal Monday."

"Does that mean you'll think about it?"

"I— What?" She heard him talk to somebody in the background. "Yeah. Listen, Max, I've got to go. We'll work it out Monday."

She ended the call, a flutter of excitement in her gut. Okay, so it wasn't precisely a yes but it wasn't a no. He was open to discussion. She just needed a little time to convince him.

Snapping her cell phone shut, Max headed back toward the auction tables.

Glory stood there, licking her fingers. "What's up?"

"Jeremy's jumped ship."

"*Jeremy?* When?"

"Today." Max felt the corners of her mouth tug

into a smile. "Which leaves yours truly as the only person at BRS who knows the project."

Glory's eyes brightened. "Are they going to give it to you?"

No guarantees, Max reminded herself. "Well, it's not a done deal, but I'm not sure what else they can do. The proposal's due in three weeks. Hal and the other partners are already doing three and four projects apiece. I don't want to jinx myself but I think they almost have to hand it to me." And it would be so sweet, so sweet.

"I'd say a toast is in order," Glory said.

"Schmoozing first, then cocktails," Max ordered.

"I knew it," Glory grumbled. "The power's going to your head already."

He stood by the windows looking out across the ballroom, still not entirely sure what time zone he was in. He'd come to the gala because he needed something to do, because if he hadn't, he would have been in bed by six-thirty, asleep by seven—and wide awake at two in the morning. He might have been standing in a ballroom in Portland, Maine, but his body still thought he was baking in the Dubai desert. Shaking his head at himself, he took a swallow of his whiskey and watched couples sway to a Percy Sledge tune on the dance floor. Perhaps it was the jet lag that gave him the faint sense of unreality, the feeling that in this place, anything could happen.

And then he saw her. And all he could think was that it was too bad they weren't building a cardiology unit instead of an oncology center. A man needed to have a place to go when he felt his heart stop.

She moved through the reception, her honey-colored hair gleaming under the lights, but it wasn't that that aroused in his mind the image of a lioness. It was the way that she walked, lithe and feline. It was in the way she glanced around the ballroom with eyes that looked as gold as her hair, as gold as the dress she wore, a long, slim column that hinted at an elegant body and afforded a glimpse of what looked like a spectacular pair of legs. There was a confidence in her stride, a subtle challenge that evoked a bone-deep response from him. Less than a week before, he'd been on the other side of the world in the desert, with its drumbeat rhythms and fierce desires. Now he stood in this glossy ballroom and felt the punch of a need as primitive as any hunger he'd ever felt.

And suddenly, he found himself wide-awake—and moving.

"Very interesting," said Paul Fischer, Portland General's CEO. He stood with Max and Glory before a mobile formed of arcs of metal with geometric shapes at the ends, each balanced so perfectly that they shifted with the swish of air from every person who walked by.

"Isn't it a little small to put into a sculpture

garden?" asked Avery Sherwin, chairman of the board.

"It won't be this exact piece, of course," Max put in.

"I hope not." Pamela, Sherwin's wife, picked up the pen that sat below the silent auction sheet. "I'm planning to buy this one."

Glory beamed. "I hope you win. I usually do much larger pieces," she added to Sherwin and Fischer. "I just brought the smaller pieces because they were easy to move."

"If you've ever been to the plaza outside the Casco Bay Credit Union building, the piece before the fountain is one of Glory's," Max told them.

"And whatever I do for the medical center sculpture garden will be designed especially for the site, of course."

"Excellent. We're looking forward to seeing your proposal." Fischer reached out to shake their hands even as he glanced over the room with a practiced eye. "Well, it was a pleasure to see you both. Enjoy the rest of your evening."

It had gone well, Max thought, watching him walk away with the Sherwins. She'd had to spend time first cultivating his assistant, but Fischer and Sherwin had ultimately given Max and Glory far more time than Max had expected. And they hadn't even asked about Jeremy. "A success, I think," she murmured to Glory.

"Is it time for that cocktail?" Glory asked.

"Absolutely. I think we should—"

"I'm sorry, I just had to come back." Pamela Sherwin walked up to circle the second of Glory's pieces. "You know, your work is really marvelous. Where do you get your ideas?"

"Well—" Glory began.

"You're the artist?" another woman interrupted, tugging her companion to a stop before a piece of steel I-beam that Glory had turned into a lacy bench. "This is incredible. How do you do it?"

Max smiled faintly. She knew how this went. Another person would stop, then another, and soon Glory would be surrounded by a collection of people destined to become fans. It looked like that toast would have to wait.

Instead, Max plucked a flute of champagne off the tray of a passing waiter and wandered along the tables of the auction to see what she'd been missing. An interesting collection, and far too tempting. The Bahamas cruise was an unnecessary extravagance, she decided. Instead, she bid on a pair of Swarovski crystal earrings she thought her mother would like and a saltwater fishing rod she hoped would encourage her father to take a little bit of time away from running the family's inn on Grace Harbor. Buying presents didn't count as an extravagance, she maintained. Even so, she'd earned the right to celebrate the good news of the night by buying herself a little something.

Debating between a spa day and a gift certificate

for her favorite furniture store, Max wandered a bit farther, then stopped and let out a little breath of pleasure.

It stood on an easel, an abstract painting in blues and greens and a flush of rose-gold. And yet not an abstract, for the washes of color formed themselves into a landscape even as she looked, a painting that evoked a feeling as much as an image: Portland's Casco Bay at sunset, with the water turned golden and the offshore breeze bringing in the tang of salt water and the cries of the gulls.

"Perfect," she murmured, already picturing it on her wall. A glance at the bid sheet had her raising her eyebrows, though. The current price would put a serious dent in her bank account. Certainly, there would be no more shopping for a few months if she bought the painting. Still, it was a long-term investment, not a pair of boots that would be out of fashion in a year. It only took one more look at the painting to decide her; she bent to fill in her initials and her bid on the sheet.

Her first impulse was to drag Glory over to admire the painting, but a quick glance showed her the artist was still surrounded by admirers. As for Max, she wanted to celebrate, but doing it at the gala felt a bit like trying to cut loose at the office. There were way too many people around who were part of the professional network in Portland, not to mention representatives of competitive firms or contractors hoping for a part of the project. Like many such events, it had turned into a constantly shifting food-chain exercise of schmoozing and being schmoozed. And after two hours, she was sick to death of it all. What she itched to do was grab Glory and head out to the Old Port for complicated cocktails and maybe some live jazz. Soon, she promised herself. Once the silent auction ended, they would be free to go.

In the meantime, she wandered over to the wall of windows that overlooked the real Casco Bay, trying on for size the idea of finally being a project manager. Just the idea gave her a thrill. She could do what was best for the project, instead of always looking for a work-around. She could talk without trying to sugarcoat her words to suit Jeremy's idea of hierarchy. She could forget about office politics and focus on creating buildings that would change people's lives.

Beyond the floor-to-ceiling glass windows, the waters of the bay turned to fire in the last rays of the setting sun. Portland might have been frigid and snowbound for much of the year, but in high summer, its beauty was unrivaled. Sure, in her heart of hearts Max had ambitions of working for one of the big international firms, designing buildings all over the world. At times like this, though, there was no place else she'd rather be.

"Here's to ya, baby," she murmured, raising her glass for a sip.

"Thanks," said a voice behind her. A male voice.

Not another contractor hoping to network with BRS, Max thought impatiently. She was done with it. So she didn't bother to turn around, just glanced back as briefly as possible.

And found herself looking back again.

He was tall and dark, with skin that spoke of time spent in sunnier climes. His face had the requisite hollow cheeks, square chin and rugged jaw that made up your average good-looking guy, but this guy wasn't average. There was something about him, a gleam in those almost black eyes as though the two of them shared some private joke, a devilish set to his mouth that was only enhanced by a Vandyke. With his swarthy skin and the gleam of gold at his ear, it gave him a vaguely piratical air. His thick dark hair was long on top and disordered as though he habitually had his hands in it. Amid the suits and tuxedos, he wore a black jacket over jeans and an open-collared violet dress shirt.

Definitely not a local contractor.

Out of ingrained habit, Max glanced at his left hand and found it bare.

"Don't you know it's rude to interrupt when a person's talking to herself?" she asked.

"Sorry, I didn't realize it was a private conversation. Are you finished or do you need more time?"

Her lips twitched. "I think we're good."

"That's a relief." He stepped up beside her.

Max was used to standing eye to eye with men but she found herself tilting her chin to meet his gaze. He had a rangy build, broad shouldered without being bulky. “Fleeing the networkers?” she asked, glancing over her shoulder at the ballroom.

“Admiring the view,” he replied. But when she looked back, she found him watching her.

“The bay is that way.” She pointed toward the windows.

“I know.”

For a moment, she felt oddly breathless. Silly, Max told herself. She’d heard plenty of lines in her life and this was just one more. Except it seemed to be coming from a guy who studied her as though he knew some special secret. And she couldn’t help but look at that mouth and wonder how he kissed.

She gave herself a mental shake. “Well, if you’re going to admire the view outside, you’d better look fast. The sunset doesn’t last long around here.”

“It takes a while to get to it, though. I forgot how far north Portland is. Nine o’clock at night and it’s practically broad daylight.” Outside, the water threw up glints of gold; the islands of Great Diamond and Little Diamond glowed beyond.

“You’re not from here, are you? I didn’t think you were a Mainer.”

“No?” He studied her. “What gave me away?”

Her mouth curved. “Where do you want me to start? Not knowing when the sun sets, for one.”

“Do you keep track of it?”

“Keep track of it? If I had my way, we’d celebrate the summer solstice as a national holiday, or at the very least a state one, since it gets dark here at noon, practically, in winter."

"Celebrate it as a personal holiday for now. Or do you already?"

Max slanted him a glance. "You mean do I go out to the woods and dance by the light of the moon with flowers in my hair?"

"You do have a way of painting a picture, don't you?"

She felt her cheeks warm. "I didn't say I actually do it."

"That's a shame. It's a pretty thought."

He looked at her with that dark, intimate gaze and for just that flicker of time, the rest of the room faded away. It was just the two of them; she was alone with a man with eyes the color of midnight.

Then the sound system crackled. They glanced over to see an expensively dressed matron with frosted hair standing at the microphone. "Ladies and gentlemen, welcome to the Friends of Portland General annual fundraiser. Just a reminder, the silent auction closes in fifteen minutes, so get in there and make your final bids. It's all for charity, folks, so be generous."

Relieved and yet somehow disappointed, Max turned toward the line of tables. "I should go check my bids."

"Bids?" He walked alongside her easily. "I guess you've been busy."

"Charitable," she corrected, the strange moment

dissipating with the distance. "Anyway, they're mostly presents." And, she discovered, mostly successful. She had the earrings by a comfortable margin. The competition for the fishing gear was closer than she'd like, but the latest overbid had only beaten her by ten dollars. She tacked on another twenty and figured she'd keep an eye on it, then turned to the painting.

It was even more arresting than she remembered, the colors more vibrant, and she wanted it even more than she had before.

"Nice." He stood beside her. "It's the bay, right?"

"The same view we were just looking at, practically. Look, you can see Great Diamond and Little Diamond island, right there."

"Are you bidding on it?"

Max nodded and stepped to the table. "I've been following the artist for a while. Tim Pritchard. His first major New York show last year sold—" Then she looked at the bid sheet and made a noise of frustration.

"I take it someone outbid you."

She shook her head ruefully. "I knew I should have stayed here and watched it. The increases were getting small enough that I figured if I made a big jump, I'd scare them all off."

"Maybe they don't scare that easily."

"Maybe they should," she tossed back. Perhaps it was the news about the project, perhaps it was flirting with an attractive stranger, but something made her reckless. She added a hefty bump to the bid. "That ought to do it. Mr., um—" she looked more closely at the sheet "—Al-Aswari had better get used to disappointment. No matter how deep his pockets are."

He stepped a little closer to glance down at the bid sheet. "They might be pretty deep."

"I'll find a way."

"Are you always so determined?"

"When I want something? Absolutely single-minded."

"Single-minded," he repeated. "And everybody else has to try to keep up with you?"

She felt her cheeks warm. The champagne, of course. "So far, no one's been able to. You never told me where you were from, by the way."

"Didn't I?" His teeth gleamed. "Dubai." He reached past her for the pen, leaning over to write on the line below her name.

Max stared at the sheet of paper. "You just bid on my painting."

"It's not your painting yet. The auction still has—" he checked his watch, "—two minutes to go. And *Sheik* Al-Aswari *is* going to get your painting. I'm not big on disappointment."

Max blinked. "Sheik?"

"Indeed."

It wasn't often that she got surprised. She shouldn't have been now, Max thought. Certainly the coloring was right. He spoke without any accent she could distinguish, but that didn't necessarily mean anything.

And sheik or no sheik, she wasn't about to let him beat her.

A slow smile spread over her face. "Sheik, hmm? Does that mean I should call you Your Highness?"

He looked amused. "If you like. But—"

"Good." Without even taking time to debate, she leaned in to scribble a new number on the sheet and slapped the pen down. "Then I believe it's your bid. Your Highness."

Behind them, the band swung into "You Can't Always Get What You Want."

"Are you used to getting what you want?" He stepped closer.

Max could feel the sudden thud of her pulse. She raised her chin. "Most of the time. And you?"

"Always." Then he took the pen and wrote a higher number on the line below hers.

He was baiting her, she knew, but it didn't stop her from reacting. "I hope you don't think I'm going away that easily," she told him.

He reached out to brush his thumb down her cheek. "I don't want you to go anywhere."

It stilled her for an instant. His touch shivered through her, setting up an answering response throughout her body. Something in her system fluttered a little then, as from a tiny vibration down deep.

Until she saw the slight curve of his smile.

The hell with her bank balance, Max thought,

picking up the pen. She wasn't about to lose the game now.

But the moment she'd stood frozen had been one moment too long. Even as she reached out for the bid sheet, it was whisked out from under her fingers. She looked up to see the monitor add it to his stack with an apologetic smile.

"I'm sorry, bidding is closed."

Max stared, openmouthed, at the rapidly disappearing bid sheets.

"I guess that means I win," the sheik said.

She turned. "You are a dog."

"Careful where you say that. It's quite an insult in Dubai."

"Your point?" She put her hands on her hips. "You stole my painting."

"I did warn you."

She set her jaw. "You're just lucky."

"No," he corrected, "I'm good. Have dinner with me."

"After what you've done?"

"I'll take you to Hugo's. You can glower at me the whole time if you want."

"On Friday night? Hugo's?" She snorted. "You couldn't get a reservation two weeks from now."

His expression was half pitying, half amused. "I'll take you to Hugo's," he repeated. "I'll even— Excuse me." She watched while he pulled out his phone and scanned what she assumed was a text message. He looked up. "It looks like I have to go. Why don't you give me your number and we can make plans for later in the week."

She thought it over as he tapped in a quick reply to the text, then put his phone away. Lecturing herself, she pulled out one of her business cards. "Max McBain," she said, handing it to him.

He glanced at her card, then looked more closely. "You're an architect?"

"Why? Do you need a palace built?"

"Maybe a bomb shelter." He shook his head. "Listen, I've really got to go. I'll talk to you later."

Chapter Two

Max stepped out of the elevator into the BRS lobby, her heels clicking on the polished, narrow-planked wood floor. In the center, a blonde sat behind a semicircular workstation of golden oak and beaten copper. Behind that rose a divider of frosted glass emblazoned with the BRS obelisk logo.

"Happy Monday, Brenda," Max said to the blonde.

"Morning, Max. Nice suit."

"Thanks." She'd worn a fitted nubby silk number with a yellow and black windowpane pattern. In architecture, clothes didn't just make the man—or woman—they telegraphed an architect's design philosophy. The job was all about the visuals, and on a day like this one, she was putting her best stiletto forward. "How did Kelly's birthday party go this weekend?"

"A sleepover with a dozen eight-year-olds and you have to ask? I'm still getting crushed Pop Tarts out of the rug in the family room."

Max grinned. "Fun, then."

Brenda grinned back. "Exhausting, but fun. Kelly loved the High School Musical charm bracelet, by the way. You'll be getting a thank-you note as soon as I have the energy to badger her into it."

"I'm glad she liked it. Until I have nieces and nephews to spoil, Kelly's going to have to be my surrogate."

"She'll be happy to hear it. So how was the Portland General benefit? Did anybody interesting show up?"

Before she could stop it, Max thought of a man with dark eyes and a devilish smile. And of that one unsettling moment when he'd traced his fingers down her cheek and jolted her system.

It didn't mean anything, she reminded herself, doing her best to ignore the little roll and shiver the memory conjured in the pit of her stomach. Chalk it up to champagne and the mood of the night. When she saw him in the light of day, the attraction would be gone. If she ever saw him, that was—so far, he hadn't bothered to call.

Which was just fine with Max. It wasn't as though she was on the lookout for a man. She didn't need the shivers, she didn't need the hassles, she didn't need the distractions. Oh, dates were fun—dinner, some cocktails, a little dancing. But it never went any further than that. They never got any deeper than her skin, she made sure of it.

And always, always, she was the one who walked away.

"The gala was all right," she said aloud. "There was nobody special there. They had a great turnout, though. I think the medical center did pretty well, between donations and the auction." The auction where she'd lost to a man with a pirate's smile. Max dragged her thoughts back to the present. "Is Hal in yet?"

"Early. He was back there swearing at the computer when I got here."

"He's probably still jet-lagged," Max said. Or trying to figure out what to do about the Jeremy Simmons situation. "Okay, I should get to it. Don't forget to show me the photos of the party when you get a chance."

"When I get the energy."

Max winked. "I hear chocolate's a good cure for that."

"In my experience, chocolate's a good cure for everything," Brenda said as the switchboard chimed and she picked up a call.

Laughing, Max skirted the divider, passing exposed brick walls hung with renderings of the firm's better-known buildings. More than twenty-five years before, Hal and his partners had bought the Victorian-era warehouse in Portland's dilapidated waterfront area, keeping the top floor for themselves. In the time since, urban renewal had turned the Old Port section fashionable and the BRS building had become among the city's most sought-after business addresses.

Beyond the divider, the open expanse of the office spread out before her. And as always, the exhilaration hit, that sense that she could breathe deeper, stand taller. Good architecture could do that.

Sunlight flooded in through the rows of enormous windows on either side. The ceiling soared fifteen feet overhead. In the center, long white tables topped with brushed aluminum lamps and sleek flat-panel displays provided workspace for the draftspeople and interns, the lower-level engineers and design architects. Offices and conference rooms lined the perimeter of the back half of the floor, their frosted glass walls making them look more like glowing cubes lit from within.

She headed toward her office. Okay, so it was small and in a nook that had no window, but it did boast a door. And with Jeremy leaving, maybe she could trade up for his office. After all, she'd need the extra space if—

"Max."

She turned to see Hal stepping out of his corner office, a lean, energetic man with a white brush cut and startlingly blue eyes. As always, he had dressed impeccably. Which didn't hide his fatigue, Max saw.

"Morning, Hal," she said. "Welcome back."

"Thanks. Stop by my office when you get settled—let's say, in ten minutes. I want to go over the Portland General project."

This was it, Max thought, nerves tightening her stomach. For all that the situation seemed promising, she knew it was a long shot for someone of her age and experience to be named project manager. Except for the wunderkind, advancing in the profession of architecture was a notoriously slow process.

But her experience went beyond the seven years she'd spent at BRS, she thought as she stashed her purse in her desk. One way or another, she'd been working in architecture since junior high, when her parents had added a wing to the family's inn. It had fascinated Max, watching the project go from a few sketched lines to rooms she could walk through. She'd followed the architect everywhere, haunting him until he'd begun to allow her to work for him a few hours a week. As she'd become more skilled, she'd moved from simple tasks like copying blueprints to rendering his sketches in CAD programs, and eventually taking plans and change orders down to planning offices for approval.

Getting into a top school had been easy; acing her classes had been even easier. As a freshman, she'd even scored a summer internship at a top firm. And maybe she'd pancaked there, but it hadn't had anything to do with her work. She'd learned from the experience—God knew, she'd learned—focusing twice as intensely, graduating a year early to go on to her master's degree. She'd learned and vowed to never, ever make the same mistake again.

And so here she was, potentially at the point where her career might be taking off. Max left her office, closing the door behind her. Under normal circumstances, one of the partners likely would assume command of the Portland General project. But these circumstances weren't normal. Hal and Leo were swamped with important commissions already. Someone had to handle Jeremy's other projects, several of which were in the final design stages and took priority over a mere proposal. BRS would eventually replace him, but hiring architects at that level took months. Getting someone on board by the proposal deadline was impossible.

Hal would probably take over as project manager, just for appearances' sake, Max figured as she walked. But he might just give her the post of lead design architect. She'd been licensed for going on five years. Her résumé held plenty of experience. She knew the project inside and out. All she wanted was a chance.

And then she was approaching the door, which she could see was open. Max stopped just outside of view and took a moment to run her hands down her suit, straightening wrinkles that probably weren't there. Then, with a deep breath, she took a step forward and knocked on the door frame. "Hi, Hal, how—"

She stopped on the threshold. Hal's Herman Miller

chair sat unoccupied, its owner nowhere in sight. At first glance, the office itself appeared empty, until she looked to one side to see a man in the corner, staring out the window.

"Oh, sorry," she began and froze as he turned to face her.

She'd been wrong, Max thought as something skittered around in her stomach. The light of day did nothing to take away the attractiveness. Nothing at all. Sheik Al-Aswari looked just as good by Hal's window as he had under the light of the chandeliers.

Better, in fact. Gone was the casual fashion renegade. This man looked sharply stylish in black linen slacks and a crisp, silver-gray shirt fastened up to the neck. One of the buttons in the center of his chest was red and it kept drawing her gaze. He'd trimmed the Vandyke so that it accentuated his mouth and jaw more sharply than ever. But his eyes remained the same, studying her with that same indolent amusement.

Sheik Al-Aswari, first at the Portland General gala, now in the BRS offices.

Max folded her arms. "Boy, I can't wait to hear this one."

Just then, Hal hurried up behind her. "Max. I guess your ten minutes is faster than mine. Come on in." He moved to his desk, gestured to his visitor. "I want you to meet my son, Dylan. Dylan, this is Max McBain."

If she'd been invited to offer ten guesses, that certainly would not have been among them. Hal's son? The sheik? Of course, he hadn't looked much like a sheik. Then again, he didn't look like Hal, either, nor like the fresh-faced kid in the high school graduation photo Hal kept stuck on a shelf. Dylan Reynolds. An architect in his own right, Max recalled, with an international reputation. An architect who'd just happened to show up at the gala. An architect who'd seen her card, knew she worked for his father, and had said nothing.

The slow burn started.

Max didn't believe in coincidences and she didn't much care for games. Especially games that left her looking the fool.

She turned to Dylan with a warmth only slightly less artificial than her smile. "Why, Dylan, nice to meet you. What an...unexpected pleasure. Hal has said so many wonderful things about you. Gosh, I feel almost as if we've already met." Out of habit, she reached out to shake hands with him.

Max met people in a business context all the time. She'd never viewed a handshake as anything other than a professional greeting. She'd never thought it could scatter her thoughts. She'd never expected it to weaken her knees. But there was an electric intimacy to the slide of palm against palm when her hand touched Dylan's that had her taking a surprised breath. His hand was tougher than she would have expected for a man who made his living at a desk, and stronger. He held on a few moments longer than absolutely necessary, watching her. Then Max saw the corner of his mouth twitch and visions of mayhem ran through her head.

"Welcome to Portland." She gave him her blandest professional smile and turned to Hal. "Don't let me interrupt if you two are visiting. I can come back."

"Not at all. Please, have a seat." Hal gestured to the client chair next to Dylan. "How did the gala go?"

Max took her time sitting down, crossing her legs with a whisper of hosiery. When she caught the turn of Dylan's head out of the corner of her eye, she smiled faintly to herself. Two could play the game, she thought.

"The gala went well," she told Hal. "Paul Fischer and Avery Sherwin spent quite a bit of time talking over the project with me. They liked the meditation garden idea, by the way, and Glory Bishop's sculpture."

"Good. And the proposal is due Friday after next."

"Yes. I've done a fair amount of background work and Mindy and I have been pulling some of the proposal material together. We're in good shape, I think, as long as I can tap the drafting team and structural guys."

Hal nodded. "That's why I wanted to talk to you. We made the short list for the project, but that list includes a couple of pretty heavy hitters. The New York group, in particular, has a substantial track record in the health care sector. We don't have any. We've got the advantage of being local but that will only carry us so far."

"I think we also have some design innovations to offer, and we're going all green," Max argued. "A track record can cut both ways. It's easy for them to fall into the same patterns because they've done it so many times before. We're walking in with a fresh eye."

Hal leaned forward and folded his hands together. "It isn't a matter of whether offering either innovation or experience. The winning team is going to have to bring both. Jeremy's résumé gave us health care design experience, but now he's gone. If we're going to win the Portland General project, we need a rainmaker. That's why I brought in Dylan." Hal paused. "He's going to be your new project manager."

Dylan had to give her credit, she played it very cool. She had to have wanted the spot, making his father's announcement a disappointment. And yet, the only evidence of any agitation was the faint beat of a pulse on the side of that pale gold throat.

Today, she was every inch the polished professional in her edgy suit, that tumble of glossy blond hair caught up in a clip. Her chin spoke of determination, her posture, of total focus. There was little she could do to camouflage that mouth, though. Her mouth didn't evoke professionalism. Full and soft, it was pure invitation. The indentation in her lower lip made him itch to trace it with fingertip and tongue, made her look as though every word she said was a delicious secret. Her scent drifted over to him, sandalwood and spice.

"You're a rainmaker?" Max glanced over at him. "Does that mean there's a chance of showers?"

A cold one, for him, if he didn't get focused. "If we have the right team, we can win this thing."

"Dylan designed the new surgical unit at the Parker-Woodward clinic and the biotech lab at the Carstairs School of Medicine," Hal put in. "He's been working on an office tower and resort complex in Dubai, but it's on hold for the time being. Which is a good thing for us because he gives us exactly what we lack right now. He's agreed to come on board as design principal and lead design architect."

This time, Dylan did see the reaction, a faint tightening of the muscle in her cheek.

"The man of a thousand personas," Max murmured in a tone of voice that Dylan knew was intended for his ears only. She was hopping mad, he realized. Outwardly, she appeared relaxed. Only the jiggling of her foot at the end of that lovely calf betrayed her.

Sitting in his Manhattan office the Friday before, fresh back from Dubai, the last thing Dylan had expected was an SOS call from his father. An important project, a vanished team leader and an assistant who had never won a contract solo. Come to Portland, Hal

Reynolds had said, and bring your star power with you. Dylan had imagined a skinny, midtwenties guy who still lived with his mother, not this golden, curvy woman who could make his mouth go dry with just a glance.

He'd arrived in town before his parents had returned from Munich. At loose ends, he'd seen the gala tickets on the refrigerator and figured he'd go and see what he could discover. What he'd discovered was that charity fundraiser crowds were the same everywhere: older, well-heeled, sedate. And then he'd seen Max.

She might have chosen a conservative dress but nothing about her had been sedate, particularly the glint in her eye. It had spoken of ambition, a thirst for challenge, a taste for adventure.

Of course, the glint currently in her eye reminded Dylan more of a lioness stalking her prey.

His father continued, thankfully unaware. "Dylan will be here full-time until the proposal deadline. You'll be working with him the same way you did with Jeremy."

"Of course," Max said after a beat. Her smile held something Dylan didn't entirely trust. Max was many things, but he knew already that working with her would never be easy.

"Dylan will eventually have to go back to Dubai, of course." Hal's BlackBerry buzzed and he silenced it impatiently. "When the project goes into the construction documents phase, Max, you'll be our point person here. Dylan will just consult as necessary. Any questions?"

"No questions," she said.

"Good. I know you two will do a great job. Now if you'll excuse me, I need to get this call."

"'When the project goes into construction,'" Max repeated, giving Dylan a sidelong glance as they rose. "Better get working on that rain dance, Your Highness."

Chapter Three

Cats had nine lives because they were good at landing on their feet, Max reminded herself as she punched the call button for the elevator. And as soon as she got her breath back after being sucker punched, she'd land on her feet, as well. So things had turned out differently than she'd hoped. It had happened before and she'd survived. She'd managed Jeremy and she could certainly manage Dylan Reynolds.

Assuming she didn't strangle him first.

She heard the sound of footsteps on the polished maple floor at her back. "Taking a break?" someone asked.

It didn't surprise her even remotely to turn and find him there. "Thinking."

"About the project?"

"About what constitutes justifiable homicide." With a ping, the elevator arrived.

He raised a brow. "Should I be scared?"

"Why, do you feel guilty?" She stepped into the empty car.

He followed and gave her an amused glance as he stood by the control panel. "Where to?"

"Me? Or you?" The doors rolled shut.

"Us. I'm pretty sure I already know where you'd like to tell me to go."

"Oh, but it would be so fun. Your Highness," she added. In the dim confines of the elevator, he was too close, but she refused to give in to her impulse to step back. Instead, she reached past him to push the button for the ground floor. "Does your father know that you've gone native and bought a title? Or is that just our little secret?"

He caught her hand as she withdrew it. "You were the one who jumped to conclusions."

A jolt of heat and surprise ran up her arm. Her pulse began to hammer.

Max raised her chin. "You've got my hand."

"I know." He took his time inspecting it. "No rings."

"No." She tugged but he held on. For a breathless instant, he raised her hand toward his mouth, then turned it to sniff at her wrist, inhaling her scent. "Nice perfume."

Max snatched her hand away. This time, she did

step back. Her breathing had sped up, she realized in annoyance. "So this is all my fault? I didn't make up the name. You should try for something a little better, by the way. Sheik Al-Aswari is a little over-the-top."

"Prince Muhammad Akbar Al-Aswari is a real, actual, flesh-and-blood sheik. And I don't recall ever telling you that was my name. You just assumed."

"You signed that name on the auction sheet."

"I represent some of his business interests and occasionally operate in his name. Like when I'm buying a painting I know he's going to like."

Her brows lowered. "Bad enough you stole my painting for sport but you bought it for some person halfway across the world who's never even seen it?"

He reached out to toy with her earring. "Who knows, I may keep it just for the memories."

Max batted his hand away as the elevator doors opened. "So why the whole masquerade once you realized what I thought?" she demanded as she stalked across the broad flagstone lobby toward the coffee bar in the corner. "Why not say who you were? Or is that just how you get your kicks?"

"I was there in what you would call an unofficial capacity. I figured I'd hang around, see what I could learn."

"And what did you learn?"

"A lot."

"About the project?"

"About you."

"Really." She turned to face him. "Well? Go on, amaze me."

"All right." His teeth gleamed. "You start out measured. You have a strategy, or you like to think so. But you let your temper get the best of you. You get so focused on your opponent that you forget to win."

Her amusement at his initial words turned into annoyance. "You should be careful about making snap judgments. Iced coffee," she added to the girl behind the counter, then turned back to Dylan. "You can get in a lot of trouble that way."

"Only if you're wrong."

It was that note of laughter in his voice that got her. "You want to know what I learned at the auction?" she challenged. "You're not above fighting dirty to get what you want. You're also lucky, but you can't depend on luck all the time. It'll turn on you, especially when you get cocky."

"You decided all that at the gala?"

"That's right, during the gala, when you were busy trying to hit on me."

"Funny, I had the distinct impression that it was a mutual effort," he said.

Max picked up her drink and walked away to the little shelf that held sugar and cream. "I might have been interested in passing, but only because I didn't know who you were. Now that I do, it needs to stop."

"Really."

Max tore open a packet of sugar and dumped it into her cup. "We're going to be working together. That means that we act like professionals and get the job done. That means no more games. No more stunts like in the elevator." She turned from the counter to find him right behind her. The breath backed up in her lungs. "You're in my way." It took work to keep her voice steady.

"I intend to be," he said. "Get used to it."

He was trying to provoke a reaction, Max told herself, trying her best to ignore the fact that he was doing a damned good job of it.

"I know how to build a proposal," he said. "I've been winning contracts since before you graduated from the U of O." His mouth curved as Max's eyes widened in surprise. "Oh yes, I've checked. I'm very thorough. And I'm good. We'll win this project, I'll make sure of that. I might even refrain from touching you during business hours. As for what happens when we're off the clock, well..."

And whether it was the heat in his eyes, the nearness of his presence, the memory of his touch, Max suddenly had a very vivid picture of what could happen off the clock.

Get a grip, she told herself as she looked at that mouth. This was not about the personal. If she kept control, it could all work to her advantage. She'd managed to get her way to a certain degree with Jeremy via a well-timed smile or a bit of flattery, and Jeremy had been as dried up as an Egyptian mummy. Imagine what she could do with someone as obviously…attentive to her femininity as Dylan. Max smiled in spite of herself. Oh yes, the situation had possibilities.

Dylan studied her. "So it looks like we might be in agreement. Maybe this little partnership holds promise after all."

"You know, I think it does," Max purred. "Can I buy you a cup of coffee?"

The baseball darted across home plate and landed in the catcher's club with a smack.

"Ball," the umpire said crisply.

"Oh, come on, ump, ring 'im up," begged a fan.

Dylan sat behind home plate at Portland's Hadlock Field and watched the hometown Portland Seadogs battle it out with the Harrisburg Senators. The arc lamps flooded the grass and red clay of the field with light. Hot dogs and popcorn scented the air. In the row ahead of Dylan, a young daughter sat in her father's lap, energetically waving a puffy hand.

Dubai had golden sand beaches, turquoise water, beautiful women and near year-round sun. The thing it didn't have, Dylan thought, was baseball.

The batter got a third strike to end the inning and the players filed off the field. The sound system swung into "YMCA." On the dugout roofs, two members of the entertainment staff led the dance while around the stadium, children stood to join in.

You had to love the minor leagues, Dylan thought.

"I see you at least kept the score reasonable until I got here," said a voice from beside him. Dylan looked up to see Neal Eberhard, his friend since fourth grade, hands full of hot dogs and beer. "Sorry I'm late," Neal added.

Dylan reached up to take the food carrier from his friend so he could sit. "No problem. I figured you couldn't get your hall pass validated."

"No, even better. We got everybody fed and I was just getting ready to go when Ronnie puked all over himself."

"Sorry to hear he's sick. Nothing serious, I hope. Or contagious."

"Nah, he just coughed too hard." Neal grinned and handed Dylan a hot dog. "He's gotten to be quite an expert at it. I think he has a future in Will Farrell films. So how'd we score?"

"Two-run double by Kalish. And the kid pitcher's looking pretty good."

"At this point, they're all starting to look like kid pitchers." Neal took a swallow of beer while the first Seadogs batter flied out to left field. "So, what brings Lawrence of Arabia back from lounging around with desert babes, an irate harem master?"

Dylan thought of the Al-Aswari project, where twelve-hour days were the norm. "The prince backing the project is having a little cash flow problem. We're on hiatus. Dad wound up short staffed on a proposal, so I figured I'd show up and see what I could do to help."

"Timing's everything." Neal took a bite of his hot dog.

It wasn't a question of timing, Dylan thought, although circumstances had certainly made it easier. The reality was, he would have figured out a way to make it happen no matter what. Especially since it was the first time his father had ever asked him for a favor.

And Dylan owed him.

In Hal Reynolds's late twenties, he'd been the boy wonder of architectural circles. He'd been at a top New York firm, working on projects around the globe. Then came love, then came marriage and then came Dylan in a baby carriage. That had led to the decision to move back to Portland, Arianne Reynolds's childhood home. For Hal, the choice between flying around the world to work on important buildings and being there to see his son's first steps was a no-brainer.

When it proved that nature had decided they would remain a family of three, that hadn't swayed Dylan's parents. Hal had already established a practice in Portland, and if it was more modest than his early career hopes, he'd never complained. So when he called all those years later, Dylan hadn't even taken time to debate before replying.

"And does the prince know you're gone?" Neal asked as the third batter hit into a double play to end the inning. “Don’t those guys kind of like having people hanging around at their beck and call?”

“The prince is too busy worrying about finances to notice I’m not at his beck and call. Besides, right now, he can’t pay his becking bills. When the money comes back, I’ll be back, too.”

“What if the money comes back before you’re done here?”

“Unlikely, but I’m working to get the proposal done as quickly as possible, just in case.” And keeping his fingers crossed, Dylan added to himself.

“Fair enough.”

A team employee dressed in a T-shirt and khaki shorts ran onto the grass to officiate a battle between people dressed in inflatable sumo wrestler costumes.

“Hey, before I forget, Sandra says come over for dinner while you’re here. She hasn’t seen you in forever and you’ve never even met the younger two kids.”

“Do they vomit, too?”

“No, that’s just Ronnie’s game. How’s next Friday?”

“Why the rush?” Dylan gave him a glance, then his eyes narrowed. “Wait a minute. You’re planning something, aren’t you?”

On the field, the sumo wrestlers took a run at each other. Neal suddenly began studying them intently. “Nope, not me,” he replied.

“Sandra, then.”

Neal squinted at the field. "They've got to be pretty danged hot in those outfits, don't you think?"

"She's trying to fix me up again, isn't she?"

"Who, Sandra?" Neal did his best choirboy imitation. When Dylan just looked at him steadily, he sighed and relented. "Well, she might have this friend from her book group..."

"Would you please tell her I don't need to be fixed up?"

"Do you think she listens to what I say?" Neal snorted. "She keeps thinking that if you just met the right woman, you'd settle down instead of living in hotels and running around exotic parts of the world that she knows I've never been to. And probably won't now until we're at least sixty."

"They're very nice hotels," Dylan told him.

"And I bet you like the exotic women, too."

Dylan raised his eyebrow. "Are you pumping me?"

"No, my imagination does nicely, I think. And if your stories didn't match up, I'd lose all respect for you." Neal clapped as the Seadogs returned to the field. "But if you ever change your mind..."

"I'll let you know."

Dylan liked women, as individuals and as a breed. He liked talking with them, watching them, being around them. He dated often, though seldom exclusively—it was hard to sustain a serious relationship when a man was rarely in the same city for more than a month or two, and he didn't believe in creating expectations he couldn't fulfill.

Someday, yes, he wanted a wife and kids. But he had things he wanted to accomplish professionally first. His father had gotten it right, Dylan figured—focus on the career first, then settle down and raise a family. For the time being, he liked living in hotels, he liked seeing the world and he liked a variety of women in his life.

Especially one woman, in particular, who made up a whole variety on her own.

"You're freakin' amazing." Neal shook his head.

"What?"

"I know that look."

"What look?"

"No wonder you don't want Sandra to fix you up. Sure, you've been here, what, three days? I bet you already have someone on the hook. Where'd you meet her?"

"Watch the ball game," Dylan replied.

Neal gave him a reproachful look. "I can follow more than one sport at a time. Come on, tell."

Dylan wasn't sure what there was to tell. He was working a tricky project on a tight timeline that threatened to shrink without warning. And success was mandatory. He had no business getting distracted by the very delicious Max McBain. But there was more to her than just her looks, he'd known that within the first five minutes. There was intelligence, stubbornness, ambition and that underlying challenge that he found downright irresistible.

A smart man would let her be, and Dylan considered himself a smart man. But he'd always been good at multitasking. No reason he couldn't build a winning proposal and still give Max McBain the time and attention she deserved.

Because she was definitely a woman who deserved attention.

Chapter Four

"When Hal said you could make rain, I don't think this was what he had in mind." Max turned toward Dylan from the window, where an unexpected summer thunderstorm pounded the glass. They stood in his office, once Jeremy's. It appeared Max's hopes of getting a window of her own were on hold.

Along with so much else.

Patience, she reminded herself. Granted, she'd found herself right back in the same situation she'd been in so many times over the years. But she'd learned to manage it. Being the power behind the throne wasn't the same as being on the throne, but she'd discovered that, with a few well-practiced tricks, it was power nonetheless. It wouldn't take much time to figure which tricks would work on Dylan Reynolds; in fact it seemed pretty obvious. She'd done it before. There was no reason to expect that it would be any different this time.

Oh yes there was.

Max ignored the mocking little voice in her head, the same way she'd ignored the little shiver that had run through her in the elevator. He'd just been trying to get a rise out of her. She wasn't about to let him succeed. The surprises were over with. From now on, she was the one in control.

She rolled a chair over from the glossy white worktable on the other side of the office to the desk with its computer. She sat, hand hovering over the mouse. "May I?" At his nod, she tapped a few keystrokes and opened up the file tree. "I put everything about the project on the company common drive—the request for proposals, the schedule, history, preliminary designs, notes. You can find it all here."

His footsteps sounded on the floor as he walked up behind her to look at the computer monitor, resting one hand on the back of her chair. The hairs on the nape of her neck prickled in awareness. Whether or not it was her imagination, she swore she could feel the heat of his body. She knew she could hear the sound of his breath. When he reached down to take the mouse, she took care to move her hand away. Not cowardice, Max told herself, just prudence. Out of the corner of her eye, she thought she saw a faint twitch at the corner of his mouth.

She set her jaw. "I think you already know the basics," she said crisply. "Portland General invited three firms, including BRS, to submit proposals for a sixty-thousand-square-foot addition to the main building. The request for proposal specifies patient rooms, treatment rooms, an infusion center, an outpatient surgical center, radiology, lab, offices, the whole deal. The new wing will connect to the structure at the location of the current main entrance, so we've got to build them a new one."

"And we've got three weeks until the deadline?"

"Fourteen days, actually. The Friday after next."

"Seventeen days." He dropped into the chair next her. "Don't forget, weekends, too."

"What if I have plans?"

"Break them." He grinned. "Until that proposal's done, you and I are going steady."

"Oh, goody. Do I get your letter jacket or your class ring? Or you could just give me back my painting."

"Can't. It's enjoying staying with me. I'll let you visit it, though, if you're good."

"I'll pass." Max reached for the mouse again. "We've got some meetings set up over at Portland General that should help us get a bead on what to deliver for the final proposal. Our in-house design review is next week, then we present the proposal and you do your rain dance."

He unbuttoned his cuffs and rolled them up. His forearms were sinewy and powerful, and as tan as the rest of him. Max dragged her gaze away.

"What's been done so far?" Dylan asked.

"Some background work and preliminary design. I've made a list of some recent health care trends we'll want to address and some code issues to keep in mind." She opened up another folder. "We can run through some of our more recent layouts and what we sent in to make the short list. I can also show you Jeremy's notes, if you like."

"Don't worry about it. I've seen his work."

Max stopped and turned in her chair to look at him. "You know, I think I could actually grow to like you."

"Admit it, you already do."

She felt a smile tug at the corners of her mouth. "Don't get ahead of yourself. So, let's see, we have a couple of preliminary floor plans in the works but they're pretty much all variations on a theme—lab and diagnostic imaging on the ground floor, and outpatient treatment, including examination rooms, infusion and day surgery on the second floor. The patient rooms will be on the third floor, which will connect with the existing surgical ward in the main building. The fourth floor features offices with a rooftop garden."

He nodded, taking the mouse from her to roam around the various plans. He sat for a moment, drumming his fingers thoughtfully. "Do you have printouts of the drawings?"

"On the wall behind you."

Dylan crossed the office to pull them down, then laid them on the worktable. Max rose to join him.

"Coming to help?" he asked.

"I'm the tour guide." As she watched, he bent over the printout, one hand holding it in place, and began to draw red crosshatching over the rooms in the center of the floor plan.

Without having spent more than five minutes looking at it, Max thought, feeling the quick whip of shock and irritation. Those plans represented months of work from the entire BRS team. If nothing else, they at least deserved a careful review before he made wholesale changes.

"If we pull all of this out of here, we can have an atrium at the entrance with a vaulted concourse that continues along the length of the addition," Dylan explained, not noticing her reaction. "It'll have seating groupings at a couple of points, maybe a water feature or two. Basically, it'll function as an elongated lobby."

"Are you aware you just crossed out the recovery area for the day surgery center?" she asked, keeping her voice even.

"So we put it somewhere else." He pulled the third floor plan over, then pushed it aside.

"Where, exactly, do you think that's going to be? We've spent weeks on these plans. All the space is spoken for."

"So we make trade-offs. You're talking about the main entrance to a major medical center. It's got to wow them." He found the floor plan for the ground level and attacked the entry area with careless red swipes. A sheaf of dark hair fell over his forehead and he pushed it back impatiently. "We also need a reception area and an information desk here."

"We already have an information desk. You'll see it if you look between all those red lines you just added."

"Not big enough." He didn't look up. "We need drama."

"We need treatment space," Max countered.

"We'll have it. Besides, if people want information before someone cuts them open, it needs to be clear where they go." He started sketching new lines on the drawing with confident strokes.

Even infuriated as she was, Max found herself temporarily fascinated watching the swift, graceful movements of his hand, the speed with which the ideas flowed from his mind to the paper. "If we cut the balcony garden outside the infusion center and move the supply room downstairs, we can still keep the recovery area on two," he continued. "What's this over here?" He pointed to an area at the back of the third floor.

"The family suites," Max told him. It had taken her two months of working on Jeremy, but she'd finally managed to convince him that it was the very latest standard of care for medical facilities and he was a genius to add them.

"Family suites? For families that get sick together?"

"In a way, yes. The new wing includes a pediatric oncology unit. When there's a kid in for an eight-hour brain surgery or stuck in intensive care for a few days, the family needs a place to stay."

"Yeah, it's called a motel."

She straightened, and all her careful strategy went right out the window. "You want to tell a six-year-old kid who wakes up crying that Mommy and Daddy are going to have to drive over from the Bide-A-Wee down the street to see him?"

"No, I want to tell the patient who needs surgery that they can get it today instead of waiting two weeks for a bed to open up because we didn't put in enough rooms. The board wants this place to be a center of excellence and that means having a certain capacity." He came up to face her. "The family suite thing is a nice idea but we can't afford it."

"But we can afford to waste all that second-floor square footage to make a hospital wing look like a shopping mall?" Max retorted. "Health care is about more than just medicine, it's about emotional support. Treat the patient."

"Listen to your client."

She took two steps toward him. "The patient *is* our client."

"No, the client is the group whose signature is on the check," he shot back. "If you don't make them happy, we don't get the contract and your patients won't get their family suites, anyway. We can't do it all—but we can do what it takes to win."

"The family suites and the infusion center gardens were the main concepts in the proposal that got us short listed. You want to take a chance on taking that out?"

"I want to make a proposal that's going to give the client what they want."

"And how do you know that, from overhearing a few speeches at the gala?" she demanded. "You haven't even been to the site. You haven't seen the medical center. You haven't talked to the staff." Her voice rose. "You don't know the first—"

"How's it going in here?" Hal stuck his head in the door.

Max snapped her mouth closed. Dylan tossed the pen on the worktable and jammed his hands into his pockets. "Just brainstorming."

"I kind of like to hear architects arguing about a design," Hal said mildly, walking over to the table as if he intended to look at the drawings but mostly studying the two of them. "It tells me they're invested in what they're doing."

"We're only talking over some changes to the floor plans everyone okayed at the last design review," Max said, watching Hal scan the floor plans.

He nodded. "It's important to have a starting point. If nothing else, knowing what you don't want will help you figure out what you do want." He pushed the drawings aside and turned toward the door. "She's right, you know," he added as he crossed the threshold. "You really should see the site. Go on over, kick the dirt, check out the exposures. Get some fresh air."

Silence hung in the air for a moment after he left. Dylan raised a brow. "The rain's stopped. Want to take a ride?"

Max let out a breath and nodded. "You drive, I'll buy coffee."

Set on a promontory southwest of downtown, Portland General Medical Center had long formed a major part of the city skyline. If form indeed followed function, the building stood as proof that the philosophy wasn't always a good thing. In the ninety-seven years since opening, the austere, four-story brick building had sprouted additions, wings and outbuildings that were successful to varying degrees, the average degree, Max thought, being not very.

"Christ, what a mess," Dylan said as he rested his arms on the roof of his car, staring across at the complex from the front parking lot.

"Design by committee gone wrong," she agreed. "That's what happens when you don't have a master plan."

Of course, even master plans didn't always work out, Max thought as they closed their doors and walked toward the building. She'd proven that to herself not half an hour before. She'd had team leaders she'd worked with—and around—seamlessly for years. With Dylan Reynolds, it hadn't taken five minutes for her to completely lose control of the situation.

His presumption needled her, his arrogance annoyed her. There was also the matter of that humming awareness that ran through her when he was nearby. It distracted her, put her off her game.

The site visit offered a fresh opportunity, she figured. They were outdoors with plenty of space between them, no more of those disconcerting tight interior spaces. It would set her free to focus on persuasion, one of her strongest suits.

The thunderstorm had exhausted itself, leaving a few ragged shreds of cloud through which the sun now streamed. They headed toward the main building, paralleling the horseshoe drive that allowed vehicles to drop patients at the front doors. The dormer windows on the roof of the main building caught the light.

Max stopped at the curb. "The addition will run from here to tee into the main building at the front doors. The footprint extends to about the third dormer window on either side wing. The entrance drive and the lot we parked in will need to come out to make room."

Dylan nodded, studying the facade. His eyes weren't black, she saw in the daylight, but dark brown with little flecks of amber. "You know, it's not her fault. Look at those proportions. Look at the detail work around the windows. The lady's got good bones.

She's kept her dignity, even if they have stuck that god-awful temporary bungalow on her front lawn. We can make this work."

"Of course we can."

"What we can do is combine a modern look with the traditional elements. We'll have to watch how we use new materials, though."

Or not use them at all, Max thought, happy to take the opening. "So you're saying we should just stay with brick?" she asked. "I like the idea. What are you thinking, jump off from the original design, maybe echo that contrast detailing around the windows?"

"Not necessarily." He began walking parallel to the building, taking long, loose-limbed strides.

Max watched a moment before chasing after him in her heels. "Weren't you the one who was just telling me she has good bones?"

"I was."

"So if I understand you right, you're thinking we should design an addition that puts the focus on that."

He threw her an amused glance. "I am?"

"I think you're smart to respect the original look. In three years, the center is going to celebrate its hundredth anniversary. Your idea will help celebrate it, too."

"Hmm." He stopped opposite the third dormer window to check the splotch of orange spray paint on the sidewalk where the surveyor had marked it.

"After all, you're right, this is New England," Max

reminded him. "People don't want flashy, they want traditional."

"Except traditional in medicine means wards of metal-framed beds and nurses with starched white caps. There's a reason medical buildings look modern. People want to know they're going to get the very latest medical care, and the building needs to reinforce that impression from the minute they drive up. It doesn't do any good to design a structure everybody loves if patients stay away."

"Well no, of course we don't have to be slavish. I'm just saying you've got a good point when you suggest that respecting the design is a good starting point. I'm sure the medical center board will like the idea."

"Really?" He slowed as they neared the end of the sidewalk at the far end of the property. "Tell me, did Jeremy Simmons fall for this routine?"

Max frowned. "What?"

"You, getting out the butter and lathering it all over me." He swung around toward her, the look in his eyes anything but amused.

She stopped. "I'm only offering an opinion."

"No, you're trying to get me to think that what I want to do is what you really want to do. I'd call it good old, garden-variety manipulation. Or at least a stab at it."

"I'm not trying to manipulate you. I'm trying to agree with you, have us move in the same direction." Even she could hear the edge in her voice.

"Sure you are. You've already decided what you want this addition to look like and you're doing your damnedest to convince me it's my idea, too." He took a step toward her. "Look, you may be smart enough to run rings around most of the project heads you've had to deal with. Hell, you may even be smart enough to do the same thing to every guy you meet—assuming you meet just the right ones. You said at the gala you hadn't ever run across anybody who could keep up with you? Guess what? You just have."

Anger pricked at her. "What makes you think you have the right to talk to me like that? I don't know what kind of women you hang out with, but I don't need to butter you up, Reynolds. Don't flatter yourself."

That pirate's smile spread slowly across his face as he took another step toward her. "I don't believe in flattery. Reality is so much more interesting, don't you think?"

"I'm not interested in your reality."

"You sure seemed like you were yesterday at the coffee bar. Or was that just about figuring out a way to hold the reins?"

"That was about getting you out of my way," she said sweetly. "And you fell for it." She turned to walk past him.

In a flash, Dylan snaked out an arm to pull her back to him. Her expression morphed from shock to alarm to fury.

"Let go of me," she spat.

"Eventually," he agreed, enjoying the feel of her, taut and curvy against him.

"Now."

"No." Not when her scent was winding into his senses, sandalwood and spice. Not when he could watch the mad beat of the pulse in her throat. Not when he could see that mouth, that soft, delicious mouth that tempted him even now.

"So you're sure you're not interested?" He leaned in deliberately, watching her eyes. They were the color of topaz, streaked with green near the pupils, a green that disappeared as they darkened. They might also have been damning him to hell, but they darkened. He could hear her breathing speed up. "It's dangerous to twist the tail of a tiger," he murmured. "You never know what'll happen."

And then he felt it, a tremor running through her, faint as the tap of butterfly wings.

Need punched through him, taking him by surprise. Suddenly, what had started out as a test of wills had turned into something quite different. Suddenly, he was testing himself—and coming up wanting. Dylan Reynolds was a man used to being in control of his desires, but for a disconcerting moment, he wasn't anymore. He could feel each breath as she exhaled, knew how little it would take to bridge the gap between them. Just one taste, he bargained with himself, ignoring the knowledge that one taste would only lead to the next. Just one, he promised, lowering his lips toward hers.

And found them pressed against the smooth skin of her cheek.

It had taken every shred of strength Max could muster to turn away when every fiber of her clamored to feel the heat of his mouth. It was worth it, though, if only to see the smug certainty in his expression wiped away by surprise. Except that hadn't been smugness she'd seen, it'd been naked desire, and it had nearly taken her, as well.

Sucking in a deep breath as though coming up from underwater, Max pushed away from him. Just a moment or two to get her bearings, she told herself. The important thing was that she hadn't let it go any further. She'd stopped him in his tracks. It didn't matter that need still vibrated through her. It didn't matter that adrenaline sloshed through her veins. Dylan Reynolds had wanted to prove something? He had. He let her prove that she was still in control.

She took a step back toward him and reached over to pat his cheek, leaning in as far as she dared. "Like I said, sugar, don't flatter yourself."

And she walked away.

Chapter Five

Predawn dark still filled the room when Dylan awoke from a dream of silky skin and sleek curves and golden eyes. Max McBain wrapped around him, Max McBain, moving against him. Max McBain, driving him wild.

And her cheek, soft against his lips.

It had stayed on his mind, that kiss that wasn't a kiss. All during the ensuing day, when they'd worked in different areas of the office on different parts of the project, the memory had distracted him—her soft curves pressed against him, the faint warmth of her exhalations, that mutinous mouth just a fraction of an inch away from his.

Her parting remark that day at the hospital had

annoyed him, as she'd intended, but it hadn't stuck with him. The touch of her cheek had. Hadn't he called her determined? Well, he was determined, too. Max McBain thought she'd shown him who was in control. She thought that she'd stopped things in their tracks.

Max McBain had made a very big mistake, because all she'd done was make him want her more.

And made him more determined to have her.

With the buzz of an angry insect, Dylan's mobile phone vibrated on the night table. He picked it up to check the display and with a sigh flipped it open. "Hello, Nabil."

"Hello, Dylan," shouted Nabil Raboud, the prince's business manager in Dubai. Nabil always spoke into the phone at top volume. "Prince Al-Aswari sends his greetings and his best wishes for your continued health."

Dylan sat up on the edge of the bed. "My best wishes to the prince, as well. How are you, Nabil?" He could picture the short, plump, mustachioed Nabil sitting behind his desk in his office, dressed in one of his Savile Row suits with contrasting pocket square.

"I am well, thank you for your inquiry. The prince, however, is concerned. It has come to his attention that the delivery of structural steel for the Al-Aswari Tower has been delayed."

A matter that should have been taken up with the building contractor, not the architect, Dylan thought.

He rubbed his eyes. "I believe the vendor is holding up shipment until they receive payment."

"Oh, the money will come," Nabil said blithely. "And when it does, so will the steel."

"Which may cause delays in construction."

Which the steel supplier was hoping to leverage to get paid more quickly. "It's an unavoidable risk."

"It is unacceptable. The Al-Razi building grows by the day. The tower of the prince's rival must not open before the Al-Aswari Vertical City and it must not be taller. The prince wishes for you to make certain."

It happened, Dylan thought. Sometimes when clients hired an architect, they began to feel proprietary. In exchange for what he considered his patronage, the prince expected that Dylan would take care of any and all problems that cropped up—whether they were his job or not. "Have you talked to Ali?" Dylan asked, thinking of the tough little general contractor.

"Oh, it is not for Ali. The prince wishes you to handle this personally."

Dylan let out a long breath. "I can try to reach Ali, but please tell the prince that until new financing is in place, more shipments will be delayed. The vendors demand payment."

"Ah, but soon it shall no longer be a problem. The prince is arranging new financing with his cousin in Abu Dhabi. Construction will proceed. So will design of the other buildings in the complex, of course. He wishes to know when you will return."

When he was good and ready, Dylan was tempted to reply. "The project is on hiatus," he said instead.

"Oh no, only construction is on hiatus. The prince says design must continue. He was very disappointed to hear that you were gone."

Nabil knew as well as Dylan that much of the design work could be done as easily in New York as Dubai, especially when no checks were going out. The prince liked to attend the occasional design meeting, though. Given that it sometimes afforded Dylan the opportunity to discourage some of the man's more impractical impulses, staying on-site made a certain sort of sense. Perhaps more important, the project employed a staff of twenty-four at Reynolds Design International, and promised to do so for some time to come. For that, Dylan was willing to tolerate a few inconveniences.

Still, he had to draw the line somewhere.

"Please tell the prince that I am helping my father but that I will return as soon as I can manage."

"Your father is ill?" Nabil asked quickly.

"No, he is fine. But he's made a request of me that I can't refuse."

"Unfinished business?"

Dylan smiled in the darkness. "Right, unfinished business," he said, thinking not of the proposal but of Max McBain's scent. Definitely unfinished business.

"Of course. I shall inform the prince. When the

financing is complete we shall expect your return. Good day, Dylan."

And he disconnected, leaving Dylan holding on to a silent phone.

An hour later, Dylan walked up the brick sidewalk outside the BRS building. There'd been no point in going back to bed to toss and turn until the alarm went off, he'd figured. Better to get in and get started with the day. The two sets of sliding glass doors opened before him.

And the first thing he heard was laughter.

It echoed through the empty lobby, bouncing off the flagstone floor. At this hour, the lights were still dim and the shops shuttered, security doors still locked. Dylan glanced around in curiosity as he stepped out of the entry area. And saw Max McBain, a wide smile on her face, standing next to a grizzle-haired janitor with his wheeled trash can.

Desire shot through Dylan right down to his toes.

His palms still remembered the feel of her curves; his body still ached for her. Seeing her now only reminded him of all they'd yet to do. She'd accused him of being cocky, but there was a confidence bordering on impudence in the angle of her head, the set of her shoulders. She was sure of herself and in control—except when she got around him. It was, perhaps, the most arousing thing he could think of.

"Dylan?" Max looked startled. "What are you doing here?"

"I'm working here for the time being, remember?"

"I mean now. It's barely six in the morning." She wore a white tunic belted over a skirt the color of new spring grass. Drops of green glass dangled at her ears. Her hair was loose and all he wanted to do was put his hands in it and fuse his mouth to hers and taste her, finally taste her. She looked fresh and alert, and more than a little uneasy.

Good.

"I woke up early. Jet lag." He put out his hand to her companion, but he kept his eyes on Max. "Dylan Reynolds."

"Oh, right." Max turned to the custodian. "Dylan, meet Carl Dunston. Don't tell Hal, but Carl's the guy who really runs the joint."

"If my dad hasn't figured that out by now, he's not as smart as I think he is," Dylan said.

"You're Hal Reynolds's boy?" Carl pumped his hand a few times. "Pleased to meet you. Getting an early start, I guess. Your daddy likes to do that, too, sometimes."

"Carl's the key master," Max informed Dylan. "The lobby might be open early, but the stairwell door stays locked and the elevators don't work until seven. If you want to get in before that, you've got to make friends with Carl."

"I'll keep that in mind," Dylan replied. "Do you often come to work at 6:00 a.m.?"

This time it wasn't Max who responded but Carl. "She'd come in at four or five if I let her. Keeps trying to sweet-talk the keys out of me but I know better. I give her the keys to this place, she'll never leave. This way, she can't get in any earlier than now."

Dylan grinned. "You're a smart man, Carl."

"I have daughters of m'own," Carl said. "I don't care how much this area has cleaned up, it's no place for a lady to be running around in the middle of the night."

Max rolled her eyes. "I've taken self-defense courses, Carl. I keep telling you, I can take care of myself."

Carl stuck his chin out stubbornly. "Nope, no matter how much she tries to persuade me—and she can be pretty persuasive—"

"So I hear," Dylan said, earning a dirty look from Max.

"—I just say no. That's what Mr. Reynolds told me to do and I'm sticking with it."

Dylan clapped a hand on the janitor's shoulder. "Good man."

The janitor nodded as he stepped into the elevator and unlocked the controls. "There you go, she'll work now. Have a good day, sir. You too, Max."

"Same to you, Carl."

Max walked into the elevator and stood at the control panel. Dylan stopped a little behind her, enjoying the hint of tension in the set of her shoulders.

"I was serious about the self-defense lessons," she said pleasantly, without turning.

"And here I left my nunchucks at home."

Ignoring him, Max pushed the button for the top floor. The elevator doors rolled shut. He did reach out then to touch her hair, letting the silky strands slip against his fingers.

Max jerked her head around toward him, but too quickly so that her cheek brushed his fingers. He let them linger there a moment before dropping his hand.

"Didn't you learn anything the other day?"

Dylan smiled. "Not nearly enough," he said. "Want to try again?"

His touch still shimmered on her skin. And for a fraction of a second, before sanity took over, her first thought was "yes."

"So why the o-dark-thirty start time?" Dylan asked as the doors opened onto the BRS lobby.

Max strode out of the elevator car and into the short passage that led from the lobby to the main office floor. "You'd be surprised how much work you can get done at this hour. There are fewer distractions. And don't start with any of your games," she warned as he turned to block her way. "I've got work to do. Some lunatic got it in his head to completely change all of our floor plans and they've got to be re-rendered before the next design review."

Mischief flickered in his eyes as he raised his hands in the air and leaned in toward her, so close that she could feel the warmth of his breath against her cheek. For an instant, her knees turned to water.

"I guess I won't play any games, then," he murmured into her ear.

It would take so little. All she had to do was turn toward him. And she was tempted, God knew she was tempted. It would put to rest the curiosity that had nagged at her for days. It would answer all the questions she had. But it wouldn't be smart. And it wouldn't be safe, she'd learned that before.

Max gave herself a mental shake and brushed past Dylan. "Excuse me, I've got work to do," she said, pleased that her voice remained steady. Even if she'd had to work to keep it that way.

She'd seen little of him since that day at the medical center, staying at her computer most of the time, working on renderings. Not that she was avoiding him, of course, she was simply focusing on getting the job done. Except she hadn't been doing that very well, either. That breathless moment when he'd lowered his mouth toward hers kept replaying itself over and over again in her head. And she couldn't help but wonder what might've happened if she hadn't turned her head.

Always before, Max had been able to see a kiss coming a mile away and decide whether she wanted to let it happen or stop it in its tracks, or even control the situation so that the opportunity never arose. With

Dylan, she'd been so preoccupied with the argument that she'd found herself caught completely by surprise and unable to stop the kiss until the very last.

And the worst part was that she knew deep down she hadn't wanted to stop it at all.

She glanced over in his direction to find him standing at the door of his office, watching her. Something skittered around in her stomach. She was going to have to be very, very careful with Dylan Reynolds, Max decided as she opened the door of her office. Very careful indeed.

Max had to give Paul Fischer credit, when it came to getting input for the hospital addition, he was nothing if not democratic. The hospital building committee included everybody from the chairman of the board on down to orderlies. Nearly two dozen people crowded into the hospital's biggest conference room to talk with Dylan and Max about what they wanted from the new wing. They jostled together on the extra chairs that had been crammed in around the table. The temperature in the room kept rising.

Or maybe it just felt that way because the only open chair that had been left for Max was next to Dylan. She had to give him credit, he knew how to impress potential clients. His silver and cobalt-blue tie fell just on the über-hip side of flashy. She would have bet money that the suit was Armani. Before him on the table sat a paper-thin, brushed aluminum laptop. He looked stylish, modern, talented and fiercely competent. And he had them all mesmerized.

If she didn't watch out, Max thought, he'd have her mesmerized, too. She set down her pen, trying to concentrate on what Fischer was saying. Something to drink, she thought, would help. As she picked up her water bottle, the cuff of her jacket caught her Montblanc and sent it spinning off the edge of the table.

Max ducked down for it quickly and found herself face-to-face with Dylan, their fingers tangled around her pen.

"I didn't realize you wanted to hold hands," he murmured, amusement lingering in his eyes as he held out the Montblanc.

Max snatched it away.

He grinned and straightened. Then, with that effortless polish she couldn't help but admire, he switched gears and looked at the committee members. "We've talked about what you need to make your jobs easier, but I'd like to get the bigger picture. What kind of impression do you want this building to give? What do you want people to think when they drive up to the medical center?"

"That they'll get the most up-to-date care available," Walt Ardsmuir, chief of surgery, responded promptly. "The main building has history but we need to bring it into the twenty-first century."

Dylan glanced at Max with a raised brow that had her resisting the urge to grind her teeth.

"So you'd like a more modern effect on the outside?"

"It'll set the tone," Fischer agreed. "It'll be the first thing people see when they come in. Make sure it doesn't fight with the look of the main building, though."

"I have in mind something that will bring the two together," Dylan assured him. "Inside, we can go with something a little more modern and open, as well. If we push the rooms on the first two floors to the outside, we can create an open concourse down the middle, for example. It will give a sense of light and space."

"Sounds very impressive," said Fisher.

"The heating bills will probably be impressive, too," the head of facilities grumbled.

"Not with the right design. We'll use energy-efficient materials, maybe even look into geothermal heating."

"BRS is accredited for green design," Max put in. "We'll deliver a green-certified structure that will minimize your operating costs. We can save you money."

"On operation, maybe. We need to know how you can save us money on the construction," said the CFO, Leighton Barnes. "Our last major building project ran way over budget and schedule. We have to get this project put out for bids by the end of the year so we can get permits and materials and be ready to start building as soon as it warms up enough to break ground."

"Then start with a firm that knows how to work around the weather," Dylan said. "BRS has been designing buildings in the northeast for thirty-two years. You'll get a team that can work with your schedule and meet your deadlines."

Down at the end of the table, one of the nurses shifted impatiently. "Excuse me?" She put up her hand. "Susan Harding, oncology. You know, we've been talking for at least half an hour here, and I've hardly heard the word 'patient' come up once." She wore a smock covered with little explosions of fireworks that matched her short red hair. And her personality, Max thought. "I know cost is important, but it doesn't matter if we get the cheapest or the most modern-looking building in the world if it doesn't let us take care of the patients, does it?" She looked around the table. "I mean, isn't that why we're here?"

Ardsmuir cleared his throat. "Well, obviously we want a design that addresses our needs—"

"Our needs? What about the patients' needs?" Harding cut in.

"We're going to have state-of-the-art treatment rooms."

"That's good, but if we're serious about this center of excellence thing, we've got to go the extra distance. There are facilities that provide all kinds of extra care options—massage therapists, counselors, support groups," she said, ticking them off on her fingers. "Emotional well-being increases patient survival rate, all the studies support that. If we want Portland General to be a center of excellence, support programs have to be a part of it."

Max put her pen down. "What about something like a meditation garden?"

"Absolutely. I mean, I know not everyone is going to be well enough to go out there but even if they could just look, that would be something. Maybe family members or staffers could help them go out."

"Family support is important, isn't it?" Max asked. Out of the corner of her eye, she saw Dylan straighten.

"It makes a huge difference, especially when patients are really ill. And the family members go the distance. Some of them spend practically every waking hour here, for days at a time. I don't know how they do it, quite frankly. I mean, all we've got is a twelve-by-twelve waiting area and I swear the chairs are out of a torture chamber. We need something better for these people."

Bingo, Max thought. "What would you say to having a few rooms where family could stay in urgent-care situations?"

Harding's eyes lit up. "That's exactly the kind of thing I mean. It's a whole new level of patient care."

"I thought I saw something about that in one of the

earlier proposals, now that you mention it," Fischer said. "How hard would that be to do?"

"And how expensive?" The CFO's voice was dry.

"It's a matter of trade-offs," Max replied, warming to her topic. "You set your priorities and our job is to make it happen."

"Very good." Fisher glanced at his watch. "I see we're just about out of time. I think we've gone through all of our concerns. Are there any questions that either of you have for us?"

"Well, I—" Max began.

"No questions," Dylan cut in, rolling back his chair as Fischer adjourned the meeting. "But someone's sure as hell got some explaining to do," he added under his breath.

"I don't know what you're so upset about," Max said, hurrying through the lobby after Dylan.

"You've got to be kidding." He stalked out of the medical center's front doors, those long strides of his eating up ground. Outside, the day was gorgeous, sunny and clear—in direct contrast to Dylan's thunderous expression.

"You're the one who was talking about designing for the client. One of the clients had concerns that we could address. I thought it made sense to throw out some ideas, particularly ones they had already seen and liked."

He rounded on her so abruptly that she almost

collided with him. "Don't you ever go against my direction in a client meeting again, do you understand me?" He stared at her a moment, expression tight with anger, then turned and strode away, leaving Max to chase after him.

"It's not like we were in the actual proposal presentation. I didn't contradict anything you said and I never promised anything."

"Your family suites are not happening." He bit off the words one at a time. "I already told you, we don't have room."

"And I told you they were on the preliminary proposal that got us onto the short list," Max retorted, weaving through the parking lot in his wake. "Clearly, Fischer saw it or he wouldn't have remembered today. Anyway, I told them it was a matter of trade-offs and prioritizing."

"Trade-offs?" Dylan gave a bark of laughter. "Trade-offs are our problem, not theirs. As far as the client is concerned, our job is to give them what they want, period. They don't care how. The minute you show them an idea they like, it's in their head for good, and if our proposal doesn't have it, you can bet they'll go looking for one that does. And you ought to know that." He gave her a scathing look. "You had no business bringing that concept up in front of the client."

"So I'm supposed to sit there and keep my mouth shut even when I know there's a way to address their problems?" Max demanded. "And what, we're supposed to cross our fingers that no one else comes up with it? This was supposed to be about brainstorming, Dylan. We need to know how they respond to the idea. We need to know what they want."

"We already know what they want—"

"Or *you* think you do."

"I know I do." He stopped at his car and swung around to face her, furious with her for breaking ranks, furious with the situation and most of all furious with himself because despite the issues at hand, all he could do was look at her mouth and want her.

She took a step toward him. "I've been working on this proposal for four months. Maybe I know something, too."

"In case you've forgotten, I'm the one who sets direction for this team."

"Team?" Her eyes flashed. "A team of one maybe. If you didn't want any input, why didn't you just ask Hal for a couple of drafting slaves? That's all you're interested in, having everything your way."

"Everything my way? You're the one who always wants to orchestrate everything. You just won't give up trying to manipulate what I think, what happens on the project, what happens between us, will you?"

"*You're* the one who won't take no for an answer," she said hotly, stabbing a forefinger into his chest to punctuate the words. "*You're* the one who's always coming on. *You're* the one who's always telling me I want something to happen between us when it should be perfectly obvious that *I'm not interested*."

"Yeah? Let me show you what's obvious." And goaded beyond his limit, he dragged her into his arms and clamped his mouth over hers.

Hot and furious, fierce and urgent. Dylan knew it wasn't smart but he just purely didn't give a damn. Not this time. He made no attempt at seduction, just gave in to the frustration and desire that had been riding him almost from the first moment he'd seen her. Her computer bag thudded to the pavement. He heard the surprised catch of her breath. He just took, satisfying himself and somehow knowing he would take her with him.

Her mouth felt as lush as he'd imagined, her taste as addictive. Licking that dip in her lower lip, he savored it, drawing it in to his mouth, tightening his teeth until he heard her faint groan.

And her arms came up around him.

He'd known the passion was there, but that was like knowing the amount of charge needed to demo a building versus feeling the explosion shake the ground as the walls tumbled down. Her mouth was greedy against his. Her fingers twined through his hair. She twisted that luscious body against him, matching him demand for demand as she did every minute of the day. It was part of her, that need to challenge, that drive to plunge heedlessly into every experience. It was the part of her that intoxicated him every bit as much as it infuriated. And just as the clash of two storms gave rise to the fury of a tornado, so their desire whirled together into a furious passion.

Max thought she'd experienced all the kinds of desire a woman could, but she'd never encountered anything like this. It stunned her, it dazzled her, making a mockery of any other arousal she'd ever felt. There was no measured embrace, no time to think. It swamped her, it overwhelmed her so that she was swept along by her own response, as though her body belonged to the moment. As though her body belonged to him.

His hands ranged over her, fusing the two of them together so that she could feel the hard muscle and sinew of that lean body against her. When he drew her head back and feasted on her throat, the warmth of his lips against her skin made her gasp. Desire drummed in her veins. Control was just a memory. It was exhilarating, delicious, delightful, divine. And she wanted more—that clever mouth everywhere on her, his bare skin against hers, those nimble fingers taking her to the edge.

But beyond the edge lay the abyss.

Max tensed, feeling a sudden surge of adrenaline that had nothing to do with arousal. What in God's name was she doing?

In instinctive defense, she brought her hands down to his chest, wanting to put some kind of barrier between them, any kind of barrier. And waited for the whirlwind to stop. When she could, she turned away, sucking in deep breath after deep breath and taking one step, then another. Because surely if she got some distance from him, even a small amount, her head would clear. Surely then this demand that raged through her would abate, this ache of desire would ease.

When she circled back, she found Dylan watching her. For an instant, she felt her body yearning toward his again.

Ignoring it, she leaned down to pick up her computer bag. "We need to get back to the office."

"We need to do lots of things." He gazed at her, eyes dark with intensity. "Just say where and when."

"How about not here and not now? Not ever," she corrected herself. "We are not doing this."

"We already are."

"No."

"Is this where you start talking about work and professionalism again?" he asked. "That's what you do when you get nervous."

"I'm not nervous."

"Sure you are. I'm not sure why. One of these days you'll have to tell me. But the next thing you're going to do is tell me to back off." He shook his head. "You know, you can pretend all you want that this didn't affect you—"

"Of course it affected me," she snapped, "but it doesn't matter. I keep my personal life out of the office. I don't do colleagues." She circled around to the passenger door.

"We're not colleagues." He followed her. "I'm on a one-time consulting gig. I don't live here and in three weeks, I'll be gone. There's no reason we shouldn't take this wherever we feel like taking it."

"Sorry to bruise your ego, but I don't feel like taking it anywhere. I'm not interested."

"No?" He moved swiftly to pin her between the car and his body, one hand against the roof on either side of her. He leaned in just a bit, pressing his body lightly against hers, staying there until against her will she began to tremble.

Until she began to want.

"I'm sorry to hear you're not interested. You'll let me know when you change your mind, won't you?"

He opened her door and turned to walk back to the driver's side, leaving her shaking with what she desperately wanted to think was anger.

Chapter Six

"You want us to do what?" Henry Singer, the stocky, sixtyish head of the BRS structural engineering department stared at Dylan across the conference table.

"Cut three months out of the production schedule," Dylan repeated.

Singer was shaking his head before Dylan even got the words out. "No way." He glanced at the stack of renderings, floor plans and spec sheets on the surface between them. "Not possible, not for a project this size."

"You haven't even looked at the summary." Dylan slid a folder across to Singer.

Singer caught it before it stopped moving and

sent it back the other way. "I know the details. I've been shadowing this project since we made the short list."

"We want to make an even shorter list, Henry," Max said from where she sat at the end of the table.

He shook his head. "A couple weeks, maybe even a month, I could do. But not this."

"Portland General wants the structure under roof before next winter starts," Dylan said. "That means putting it up for bids by the end of this year in order to break ground as soon as the snow melts."

"And doing design and engineering in less than five months? You're setting yourself up for a world of hurt."

"Well, you'd better start figuring a way around it." Dylan's voice held an edge. "Our only chance of winning this project is to bring them a proposal that will let them make that schedule."

Singer folded his arms over his chest. "I've been in this business for almost forty years. I know how long it takes to get a design specced out for build. I keep to my schedule and I'm not going to put some numbers down on paper just to get a contract when I know those numbers aren't going to be good." His voice rose.

"Are you saying you can't do it?" Dylan shot back.

Singer slapped his hands on the conference table

and stood. "I'm saying if you're not going to listen to me, then maybe you need another struc—"

"Of course we're going to listen to you, Henry, you've got more experience than the rest of us combined," Max cut in, rising to put a hand on his arm. "Not to mention the fact that you're a wizard. I mean, remember the cantilever on the front of the Casco Bay Credit Union building? Everybody said you couldn't do it but you figured out a way, didn't you? You're one of the best engineers out there. Maybe it can't be done, but don't count yourself out. If anybody can figure out a way, Henry, it's you."

"I didn't say I couldn't do it," he interrupted irritably. "I just have concerns about it."

"That's why we're talking to you. It's a big job."

"I've done bigger, but not in this time frame. There are only so many hours in a day, you know, and when you get tired, you make mistakes. We can't afford that. It's not like screwing up a drawing. You screw up here and the building comes down on people's heads."

"Right." Max nibbled her lip thoughtfully. "What if we spread the work out? We could get an intern or even hire a temp. You could offload the basic stuff onto them, free you and the rest of the staff for the trickier calculations."

He considered. "I'd need a lot of help."

"You tell us. We'll get you whatever you need. You're a smart guy, Henry. You can do this."

Henry reached out for the file that sat in the middle

of the conference table. "Let me look it over and I'll tell you what I think this afternoon."

She gave him a dazzling smile. "I knew you'd come through for us."

"I haven't figured out a way to do it yet," he warned.

"You will," she assured him. "By the way, how's that granddaughter of yours?"

Henry's eyes lit up. "Sophia? Ah, she's a pistol."

"She takes after her grandpa," Max told him as she walked him out the door. "Don't forget to send me some new pictures. My last ones are two months old. She's probably looking at prom dresses by now."

Leaving him laughing, she ducked back into the conference room to gather her files. Dylan walked beside her as she headed back toward her office. "I suppose you're going to tell me that's an example of how to work with people," he said.

"BRS isn't like your giant New York agency. We don't stand on ceremony or live for hierarchy," Max said as she walked into her office. "My way or the highway might work in Dubai, but it doesn't go over so well here in Maine."

"So I hear." Dylan stepped in after her, closing the door behind them. "What does go over well here in Maine?"

"Keeping the door open, for one," Max told him crisply, walking toward it. Dylan caught her hand in his. For a moment, she froze, but all he did was hold it.

"Thank you. You took what could have been a problem situation and you made it work."

"Henry's a good guy, and professionally speaking, he's one of the best. If you've got him in your corner, he'll work miracles for you. He just has to know you respect him."

"I do respect him. And I respect you." His gaze was steady on hers, and for once there was no mischief in it. "I looked over your portfolio. You've got talent, a lot of it."

She wasn't going to blush, Max told herself. "Does that mean I qualify to stay on the show until next week?"

"It means I appreciate the work you've been doing and I value your input," he said. "It doesn't mean I'm always going to take it, but I value it and I want you to keep it coming."

His gaze locked on hers and it was like the moment at the gala, that sense of connection, like a line of communication humming between just the two of them. She moistened her lips. "Thank you."

The telephone rang, startling them both. For a moment, Max didn't move. Then she stepped over to the desk hurriedly, her eyes still on him. "This is Max."

Telephones, Dylan thought in suppressed annoyance, were an overrated technology. He was sure of that an instant later when her face lit up.

"Oh, hey, sweet thing." Lips curved in pleasure, she sat, all her attention focused on the telephone.

Then she laughed. It wasn't like the freewheeling peals of laughter the morning he'd seen her with Carl. This was the husky, intimate laugh of a shared joke and a shared life.

A strange, uncomfortable little twinge ran through him as he stepped outside and closed the door to give her privacy.

"Of course I can meet you, honey," he heard Max say as he walked away.

And Dylan Reynolds realized that for the first time in his life, he was jealous.

Summers, Max thought, were entirely too short in Portland. And she hadn't been doing nearly enough to take advantage of this one. She sat at the little metal table at the edge of the outdoor café by the doors of the BRS building, savoring the feel of the sun on her shoulders. She'd spent so much time working on the Portland General proposal over the past weeks that she'd practically ignored the fact that the warm weather had arrived. No more. As soon as the proposal deadline passed, she was going to make it a point to get out as often as possible.

Of course, she had actually been outside a couple of times in the past week and a half. But weather had been the last thing she'd focused on.

Dylan Reynolds was beginning to become an issue, she reflected as she took a sip of her iced tea. Part of the problem was that she liked him. It wasn't just that moment in her office, it was a whole host of moments added up. But it was more complicated than just liking, because above all there was the kiss, that terrifyingly, deliciously wonderful kiss that had emptied her will and left her dizzy and weak with longing for him.

Max stirred the tea with her straw to form a little whirlpool, watching it deepen. Sometimes, Dylan infuriated her with his assumption that all he had to do was touch her to take her over. Especially since it was frighteningly close to the truth. Like a whirlpool, that type of desire could swallow a woman up. And if she weren't careful, she might never get her head back above water. Max had been through it once before and it had almost destroyed her. But she knew better now.

And hadn't she shown him—and herself—that it didn't have to be that way, that she could manage her feelings and respond as she chose? Why couldn't he accept that? How many times did a woman have to turn the man away before he got it through his head? Was it just his innate cockiness that made it impossible for him to believe a woman might exist who didn't want him?

Max scowled into her tea. All right, maybe she did want him a little. No great surprise there. He was attractive. And she was attracted, but it wasn't the first time in her life and it wouldn't be the last. As strong as the attraction was, she didn't have to follow it. She could decide what she wanted and act accordingly, she'd demonstrated that already. And now that she was on her guard, he wouldn't get to her again.

"Hey, baaay-be," sang a voice and Max glanced up to see a little redhead in jeans and a pale green T-shirt.

"Cady!" Max rose to hug her younger sister. "Good to see ya."

"Good to see you." Cady kissed Max's cheek. She sat, checking her watch as she did. "Don't let me lose track of time. The meter only gave me an hour."

Max made a face. "Sorry I had to make you come down to parking hell. It's just that I've got a two o'clock meeting I have to get back and prep for."

"That's okay, we'll just eat fast. It's not like we aren't going to see each other this weekend, anyway."

Max flagged down the waitress, who stood by while they hastily selected their meals and whisked away, promising that the food would arrive yesterday.

"I hope she's serious about that," Cady said. "I'm starving."

"Like that's news? So tell me, how are plans going for the wedding of the century?"

"Wedding?" Cady grimaced. "I'm about ready to just elope."

"That's kind of a drastic decision."

Cady took a swallow of the Coke the waitress brought her. "It's driving me crazy. You wouldn't believe all the stuff you've got to do to put on a wedding."

"Your parents own an inn and your fiancé runs the restaurant. It can't be that hard."

Cady eyed her. "That's what you think. It should be easy, right? A guy, a girl, some vows and dinner, right? Wrong. This weird thing happens. You start out with a list of five things, you cross one off and next time you look, it's ten things long. And it gets even longer the next time. We have to pick flowers, we have to pick corsages, tablecloths, a song for our first dance. Pearl earrings. And invitations. Do you know you even have to pick the color of ink to use on the invitations?" she demanded. "Tell me why, in the name of God, anyone gives a hoot what color the ink is on their invitations."

Max fought keep from smiling. "Um, because their guests might be colorblind?"

The waitress brought their food, a spinach salad for Max, and a hoagie for Cady, who seized it and took a sizable bite. "And don't get me started on the wedding dresses," she continued after swallowing. "Do you know that you have to actually make an appointment to go in and try on wedding dresses? An appointment to go shopping," she repeated, affronted. "So I finally get in there and I almost run away because there are, like, fifty million dresses. But I stick it out—"

"Very brave of you."

"Thank you. I find a dress to try and I go to the

changing room. And the clerk comes in all upset that I did it on my own and insists on coming in with me. In the dressing room! I'm standing there in my underwear and she just marches in and gets the dress all bunched up to lift over my head."

She'd keep a straight face if it killed her, Max told herself. "What did you do?"

"What do you think I did? I grabbed my shirt and jeans and got out. Except that the sash of the dress had gotten hooked to me, so she was squawking and grabbing at me as I went...."

Max made a strangled noise.

Cady narrowed her eyes. "Are you laughing?"

"No." Max struggled to keep her face from twisting.

Cady glowered. "You're laughing. I'm telling you about what is possibly the most traumatic experience I have ever had in my life, being terrorized while I was completely defenseless, and you are *laughing*."

Max lost it then, flopping back in her chair and cackling until tears streamed from her eyes. After a moment, Cady joined in.

"You should've seen me, trying to walk out of there. I still had the veil on and they were running after me, waving their hands." She took a meditative bite of her sandwich. "I guess I'm not going back there again."

"You think?" Max dabbed at her eyes. "But listen, nothing says you have to go through all that hoopla just to get married."

"That's right." She brightened. "We could go to Vegas."

"Seriously, please don't. I really think that would hurt Mom and Dad's feelings. They're so looking forward to being there. I mean, when Walker got married, Elise barely let us show up at the ceremony. Mom and Dad want to be a part of this."

"I know," Cady said.

"But nothing says that it's got to be the full production in three-part harmony," Max reminded her. "If it's getting to be too much, scale it back. Invite just the immediate family. Do it in the afternoon. Wear jeans, serve cake."

"I'm marrying a James Beard award-winning chef. I can't serve just cake."

"Okay, but it can still be small."

"I suppose, but there are people I'd like to have there and people Damon would like to have there."

Max's lips twitched. "And the jeans?"

"I want to look nice for him."

"So what you're telling me is you're really just here to complain."

"Well, of course." Cady grinned. "Mom and Tania have threatened me with duct tape if I don't stop ranting."

"And Damon?"

"Damon has other ways of keeping me quiet." Cady gave a bawdy wink. "I showed up because I needed a fresh victim."

"Lucky me. Well, vent on. And if I can help in any way, let me know."

"Help me find a dress," Cady responded instantly.

"Not if you're going to go running around the dressing area in your underwear."

"Seriously, Max, I need you. You've got the shopping gene."

Max frowned. "What's that supposed to mean?"

"You know." Cady flapped her hands. "I go into a store and nothing fits and it's all ugly and overpriced. You go in and walk out with a pair of beautiful, fully lined designer wool pants that were originally three hundred dollars and then got marked down, then priced at half off and put on the sale rack and with the store coupon and the two-for-one offer, you got them for a buck fifty."

"And you think that happens by accident?"

"I think it's an inborn talent, like having good balance or being double-jointed."

"Practice, darling." Max patted her hand. "It's a matter of practice."

Cady sighed. "I just want to look nice for him."

"I've seen the way the man looks at you," Max said. "You could wear a gunnysack and be beautiful for him. He's crazy about you."

"You think so?" Cady beamed.

"I know so."

She shook her head. "It's funny, until Damon came along, I'd about given up on the whole bunch of them. I figured I'd never get married. But you always told me it was just a matter of finding the right guy. You always said the right man could change everything."

"Really," said a voice behind them. "That's interesting."

And Max turned up to see Dylan standing there.

He wasn't going to let the phone call get to him, Dylan had told himself when he'd walked away from Max's office. He certainly wasn't going to wonder who she was talking with or plumb to see if she had plans that night. It was none of his business. He didn't like jealousy. He didn't want any part of it.

The problem was, jealousy seemed to want to be part of him, lodging in him like a splinter he couldn't quite get rid of.

He'd done his best to focus on work, reviewing drawings, writing elements of the proposal, fielding meeting requests. Finally, when he found himself getting up once too often just to circle the office and get rid of his restlessness, he'd decided to go out—take a walk down to the waterfront, grab a sandwich on the way back. A change of scenery would do him good.

Of course, the last time that he'd gotten a change of scenery from the office, he'd walked away with an itch that he'd yet to get rid of. The last thing he needed to do was make it worse by stopping by Max's office. Instead, he'd headed straight out, only to see

Max sitting with another woman at the café just outside the doors of the building. And that quickly, the splinter was gone.

The itch, however, remained.

Max looked up at him. "Can't I get a break from you for even a minute?" But the corner of her mouth curved up as she said it.

It gave him the urge to kiss her. Again. "Admit it, you missed me."

"How can I miss you when you won't go away?"

He cocked his head at her. "So you think the right man can change everything, huh?"

"Emphasis on 'right,'" she said.

The other woman at the table cleared her throat.

And Dylan was delighted to see Max's cheeks redden. "Ah, Dylan, this is my sister, Cady. Cady, this is Dylan. He's running a project I'm working on."

"When she lets me," he added.

"She can be bossy," Cady agreed as they shook hands.

Max gave her an accusatory look. "Whose side are you on?"

"The same side as all right-thinking people," Dylan told her.

Cady looked from one to the other and smiled widely. "Dylan, would you like to join us for lunch?"

Max threw her a murderous stare. Cady smiled blandly.

"He's going somewhere," Max told her.

"It'll keep." Dylan pulled out a chair, enjoying himself. "By the way, the reason I came over was to tell you our two o'clock meeting shifted to one."

"Maybe we should just get the check now," Max suggested as the waitress approached.

"We've got plenty of time," he told her and ordered coffee. "Besides, I haven't even gotten a chance to talk to your sister. Are you here visiting, Cady?"

"Just for the day. I'm up from Grace Harbor."

"That's practically commuting distance."

"You know it?"

"Sure. When I was a kid, my parents and I used to stop there when we sailed down the coast. There was a restaurant by the marina that made killer clam strips."

"That's ours," Cady broke in delightedly. "I mean, my family's. My parents own the inn and the restaurant, and my cousin owns the marina. We grew up there."

"No kidding." He looked at Max in amusement. "I guess that makes you a small-town girl."

She gave him a haughty stare. "As much as growing up in Portland makes you a big-city boy."

Dylan's coffee appeared and he took a swallow. "Is it as beautiful there as I remember? It used to be a very small town, very green, not a ton of houses."

"That sounds about right. It's built up a little bit more than it used to be," Max said. "Nothing stays the same."

"You're right. Things have a way of changing on

you, whether you want them to or not." Something in the way he looked at her made Max think he was no longer talking about Grace Harbor.

She shook it off. "The inn's definitely different. There's a Michelin-starred chef in the kitchen now."

Cady grinned. "Yeah, he does deconstructed clam strips—a shucked clam next to a little pile of cornflakes. Makes it look fancy enough that he's got people happily dropping fifteen bucks for it." She shook her head. "This restaurant gig, it's a racket."

"I'll have to remember to drag my parents down to Grace Harbor when I come back to visit in August."

"Come down this time," Cady countered. "We're having our annual Fourth of July clambake this weekend."

"I'm sure Dylan has better things to do," Max interrupted.

"I'm sure Dylan doesn't." He returned her dirty look with a sunny smile. "My parents have a long-standing date with some friends down in Florida, so I was just going to hang out. A clambake sounds just about right."

"Maybe you can get a ride down with Max." Cady's eyes danced with mischief.

"Maybe I can," he agreed. "What do you say, Max?"

Gritting your teeth too hard could break them,

Max reminded herself. "Why, of course, Dylan, I can't think of a thing I'd rather do."

"Then I guess it's a date. Are you going to have fireworks?" he asked.

"Of course," Cady told him.

"Might get kind of interesting, all that fire," he said, gaze on Max.

"I always find a bucket of cold water puts it right out," she said silkily.

"You don't want to get too cocky about that. Just about the time you think you've got them all doused, you find out one's still smoldering. And that one usually winds up making the biggest bang of all." He rose. "Cady, it was very nice to meet you. I should be getting back. And, Max—" he paused "—I'll be looking forward to our ride."

Chapter Seven

There was always something in the air the day before a holiday weekend started, Max thought as she crossed the office. An undercurrent of excitement, or anticipation. Even she felt it, despite knowing that she'd be working the next day, and the next, until the proposal was finished.

The price of dedication, she thought to herself as she knocked on Dylan's open door.

Dealing with him was the price of dedication, too.

At the sound of her knock, he pushed back from the desk and swiveled the chair to look at her, taking his time. Max's cheeks warmed. It was the casual Thursday before a three-day weekend. With the temperature set to spike in the high eighties, she'd chosen a sleeveless turquoise dress that buttoned down the front. It wasn't from her office wardrobe but it was still fairly demure, or so she'd thought when she'd pulled the outfit from her closet that morning. Now, the above-the-knee hemline seemed far too short.

"You wanted to see me?" she asked.

His teeth gleamed. "Always."

"About the proposal," Max reminded him.

"That, too. I have good news, I think. I've gone over the plans and we can include your meditation garden. The only problem is that it's going to have to go on the grounds outside of the addition."

"I see." She didn't, not really, but she figured she'd hold off for the time being.

"We can't do the balcony gardens—there's just not enough room—but patients can see the outside garden from both the rooms and the infusion center. Plus, anyone who's able to get out of bed could always go down to it."

Assuming they could dress. Assuming they weren't tied to IVs and equipment. Assuming it wasn't cold or raining or worse.

Max took a breath. "I'm glad you agree that the garden concept is important. It's really going to—"

"Hold on a minute."

She blinked. "What?"

"What's in your hand?" He narrowed his eyes as

though looking more closely. "Is that butter you're holding?"

Max rolled her eyes. "I was not about to butter you up."

Dylan leaned back and folded his hands behind his head, propping his feet on the desk. "Really? Because it sure sounded an awful lot like you were starting in again."

The corner of her mouth tugged. "What I was going to say is that I think having the gardens outside the infusion center and the rooms is really important for these patients but if we can't do it, we can't do it."

He looked at her suspiciously. "Okay, what have you done with her?"

"Who?"

"Max McBain. I know you've done something with her because she sure as hell would never have been so direct, let alone accepted that she couldn't get her way."

"You know, with just the right push, I bet that chair would go right over backward," Max told him pleasantly.

"That's not very friendly."

She tilted her head. "You're my boss. Just how friendly do you want me to get?"

His eyes darkened. "Careful asking me a question like that in the office, darlin'," he drawled.

She made a move toward the chair and he sat up

quickly. Max laughed. Just then, there was a rap on the door frame.

It was Hal. "Stop by my office in about five minutes, you two," he said briefly. "I want a quick status update on the project."

Max and Dylan looked at each other as Hal walked off. Dylan shrugged. "When the bossman calls…"

A few minutes later, they sat in chairs before Hal's desk. He glanced over from his computer. "The proposal deadline is a week from tomorrow. How are things going?"

"Making progress," Dylan said. "We'll be ready."

Hal smiled briefly. "I've been hearing less shouting, so I figured it was a good sign."

Max counted herself fortunate that he wasn't aware of the other things that had been going on between them.

"We're finalizing the exterior concepts," Dylan told him.

"We've got basic renderings going of everything he's working on, which we've been updating as we go," Max said. "The sample floor plans are done, and Eli and Grant are working on the animations."

"All the bells and whistles?" Hal asked. "You know the other two teams aren't going to miss a trick. Make sure our guys include sound effects, and I want the motion to be so realistic it gives them vertigo."

"We'll do our best to make sure that everybody on the committee is swooning afterward," Max assured him with a smile. "As far as the paperwork goes, Mindy's on the case. She'll get the packets bound and keep us on schedule the day of."

"Mindy was probably General Sherman in a previous life," Hal told Dylan. "She'll send you out the door on time and with the right documents in your hands, and God forbid if you cross her. When's the design review, again?"

"Monday morning," Max said.

"Kind of late in the process."

"It would have been tomorrow but we've got the holiday and we're not ready today."

"We'll still have four days to address any comments or ideas that come up in the review," Dylan reassured him. "We'll have enough time."

Hal smiled faintly. "You should know that you never have enough time."

"We do still need to make a decision about the art for the meditation gardens," Dylan said.

"Is there a problem?" Hal asked. "I thought you were using that Glory Bishop."

"Jeremy Simmons was. I'm not so sure."

Max frowned. "Why not? She met Fischer and Sherwin at the gala. They liked her work."

"I'm not convinced she's the best choice." Dylan shrugged. "She's not all that well established. I like the idea of metal sculpture but what I saw at the benefit was mostly Calder knockoffs."

"If you take a look at her portfolio, she does far more than mobiles." Max kept her voice cool, resisting the urge to leap to Glory's defense. This was not the place for personal feelings. Of any kind. "It makes sense to stick with Glory. BRS has used her on at least five projects I can think of in the past. Besides, we've got most of her part of the proposal set."

"If your Mindy is as good as she sounds, she can pull together a CV and some photographs on a new artist by next Friday," Dylan countered. "And using Glory Bishop because you used her before is the worst possible argument. The last thing we want to do is walk in pushing an artist they've seen already all over town. It'll make them question whether all of our ideas are tired."

"Make up your mind, either she's not established or she's overexposed," Max said tartly.

"Maybe she's both," Dylan shot back. "I'm not going to—"

"Enough." Hal's voice was sharp. They both subsided and looked at him. "Have you met with her or reviewed her portfolio?" he asked Dylan.

"Not yet," he admitted. "I've been focusing on the building."

"Then do your legwork. Go out to her studio, talk to her, make a decision. But you'd better do it fast because you don't have a lot of time. Anything else?"

They looked at each other and shook their heads.

"Good." Hal turned back to his computer. "Then get to it. The clock's ticking."

* * *

"Just how far out of town does she live, anyway?" Dylan grumbled as he drove up the narrow country lane. Overhanging oaks dappled the pavement with shadow. Split wood fences lined the road on either side. Beyond lay green pasture and in the distance, a white farmhouse.

"We're almost there," Max told him. "You'll know when."

And then he saw them, a trio of exuberant white figures standing out in the field, except that they were doing anything but standing. Cartoonishly proportioned with outsized heads and hips and tiny feet, they looked like dancers caught in an instant of celebration, pirouetting, rising on one toe, or throwing their arms out ebulliently, their long hair streaming.

"You were asking before about whether we danced in the moonlight to celebrate the solstice," Max said.

"I was thinking more of live people."

"They're alive, too, just in their own way."

Closer to the house, he saw more sculptures, this time abstract, freeform pieces of metal and stone, or stacks of geometric shapes in primary colors, sharply vivid against the summer green grass.

He turned into the drive, rolling to a stop in the graveled yard that lay before the clapboard farmhouse.

The scene was bucolic, with the red and white barn, the fences, the green of the pasture and the enormous oaks that stood at the edge. Purple and red pansies nodded in the flower boxes on the porch railings and a marmalade cat lay curled up on the cushions of the glider. A pair of red hens scratched around in the dirt.

It was the perfect farm scene, except for the incongruous sight of a figure in a welding helmet and fireproof apron cutting into the bottom of an overturned water trough with a blazing torch.

"The artist in residence, I presume?" Dylan asked.

They stepped out of the car and into the warmth of the afternoon.

"Glory," Max called and shut her door. When Glory didn't respond, she gave an earsplitting whistle.

Dylan whipped his head around to stare at her. "Was that you?"

Max grinned. "One of my many talents."

"I can hardly wait to discover more. You'd come in really handy in Manhattan." He ran a hand down her arm.

Just then, Glory turned toward them, switching off the welding gun and setting it aside. In a practiced move, she pulled off her helmet, then removed the earbuds from her music player. "Wow, is it one-thirty already?"

"Closer to two," Max told her.

Glory shoved her thick gloves in the pocket of her welding apron. "No wonder I'm hungry. I've been out here since about ten. I was supposed to get finished and cleaned up before you got here, but..." She wiped her hands on her jeans and stuck one out toward Dylan. "Glory Bishop."

"Dylan Reynolds," he said, shaking it.

Glory studied him a moment, flicking a glance at Max. "So," she asked Dylan, "you're running the show?"

"In a way." He turned toward the water trough. "Are you attaching anything or just cutting away metal?"

"Cutting. It looks like hell now but it'll be gorgeous when it's done. Although it won't do a damned thing to hold water, will it?" She grinned. "Oh well, you know what they say about eggs and omelettes."

Dylan looked up from the water trough. "I like the pieces in the field. The white ones, especially, make quite an impression. They're like a celebration."

"Ah, the dancers," Glory said. "That's because I started making them on the first really warm day we had after a nasty winter."

"If you can make inanimate materials show joy, what about hope or strength?" he asked. "Do you have ideas about how to do that?"

"You mean for the hospital? It'll depend on what I come away with after I visit the place and talk to the people. I don't like to get too far ahead of myself. I have been thinking about it, though. I've made some sketches." Glory swiped her forehead with her arm. "Hey, guys, I'm dying in all this gear. Is it all right if I run in and change really quick? I'll get the sketches and bring us something cool to drink while I'm at it. No, stay out here in the shade," she advised, as they moved to walk in with her. "There's no AC inside. At least out here, you've got a breeze. Look at the sculptures, if you want. They beat the hell out of portfolio photographs. A couple of pieces down here are portraits," she added as she darted up the front steps to the house. "See if you can figure out which one is Max."

Dylan watched the house's front door slam and turned toward the gate to the field.

"You aren't really going to go out there, are you?" Max asked.

"With a challenge like that, how can I not?"

The grass in the pasture was calf high, dotted with tiny pale yellow and lavender wildflowers. A fat bumblebee buzzed on a zigzag path as though drunk with the heat. Nearby, one of Glory's mobiles sat high above them on a metal post. Only one of its vanes moved in the quiet air, shifting lazily an inch or two to the side. Farther on, red metal cubes the size of milk crates were piled into an irregular stack like the building blocks of some careless child.

Dylan turned to glance at Max. "I assume this isn't you, right?"

When she just stuck out her tongue at him, he grinned and kept going.

Ahead of them, a piece of rough carved granite rose up and curved slightly into a crude point. The edges of a series of blue glass discs projected out of it, each a few inches below the next. With the overhead sun, the discs cast blue shadows over the rock, making it look like streaming water, as though it were the front of a wave.

"Not you, either, but nice," Dylan said, turning to her.

Max slanted a look at him. "How do you know any of them are me? She could've just been joking."

"She wasn't. You have the sort of face that would fascinate an artist." He reached out and caught her chin. "Oh, not so much because it's beautiful but because it's interesting. Your face changes with every minute, every thought, every shift of the light. It's like watching a waterfall."

She could feel her pulse speed up. Strong yet gentle, his fingers spread warmth into her skin. There was something hypnotic in the tone of his voice. And she found herself helpless to do anything but watch him as he stepped closer and slipped his fingers into her hair. "Like silk," he murmured. "Almost as soft as your skin."

He leaned in toward her and she felt that shiver and roll in her stomach as she waited for the touch of his mouth on hers. Instead, he brushed a kiss over her forehead. "Almost as soft," he repeated.

And walked on. Max stood for a moment, lips parted. He hadn't really done that, had he—mesmerized her with just a few words, left her standing dumbfounded and waiting for his kiss? *Get your guard up.* She gave her head a quick shake like a dog shaking off water, then turned after him.

He'd stopped before a series of granite columns set tightly together to form a solid barrier with a lintel on top. He glanced over at Max. "I suppose this one could be you. A wall wants its own way, doesn't it," he mused. "It wants to direct people, control who gets in and who gets out."

"Lucky me, another personality assessment," she said. "Of course, if you really think I am a stone wall, just remember, rock is notoriously hard of hearing."

"Of course there's more to you than that." He circled the piece as he talked. Abruptly, he stopped, his expression first surprised, then amused. "How about that? If you look at it just right, the wall turns into a gate. I mean it, come see." He stood her in front of him and stretched an arm over her shoulder to point. "Now the columns look like slats and that little knob looks like a latch," he murmured in her ear. "It's a little bit ajar, so it can let in new ideas. Or people."

She stared blindly ahead as he settled his palms on her shoulders, feeling only the warmth of his touch, every hair on the back of her head prickling with awareness. "That could be your portrait, Max. It could be you, that wall, that gate." He nuzzled his lips against her neck for a fraction of an instant and she felt a tug in her belly. "It could be you," he whispered, "but it's not."

This time, he caught her hand as he moved on and she found herself following.

"Nope, nope, nope," Dylan kept saying to himself as they passed one piece after another. And then he stopped. "Bingo. That's it."

It came up out of a rough-cut granite base, a graceful, sinuous band of steel that rose in a shallow S-curve higher than their heads.

And she stared at him, stunned. "How did you know?"

"Look at it. It's you, exactly. It's grounded in something very solid. It's made of steel, which means that it may be slender but it's strong." He drew her around to the other side. "Funny thing about steel, it can hold things in place, but it also gives. Look at the way it curves, it's graceful. There's a softness about it that you see the longer you're around it." He turned to face her, drawing her to him with her hands. "Oh, yeah, it's you." His gaze was dark on hers, intense as he reached up to stroke his fingers over her cheek.

Max stared at him, in the quiet of the summer afternoon, held by the simple contact. Her heart began to hammer. He'd stared at her once as though they were the only two people in the room, made her feel it. And in this moment, everything else fell away. All that mattered was the two of them standing there. She might have resisted him over and over, but like the steel, now she gave.

"Open the gate, Max," he whispered. "Kiss me." He pressed his lips to her forehead. "Kiss me." He brushed his lips over her cheek. "Kiss me." He leaned in toward her, his lips a hairsbreadth from hers. "Kiss me."

And bridging that narrow gap, she did.

It was as different from that fierce, heedless kiss they'd shared in the hospital parking lot as water was from fire. This contact was all lazy warmth and quiet persuasion in the soft summer sunlight. Cicadas droned somewhere nearby. The scent of grass and wildflowers rose from the field around them.

She should think, Max knew she should think, but she couldn't with his lips so soft and warm on hers, the gentlest of caresses, teasing a response from her. Instead of dragging her into desire, he had her melting with it, the muscles in her legs softening with the urge to simply sink down onto the soft grass and lie with him.

She'd promised herself she would keep control, but how could she with this gentle seduction that tempted her into an answering response? It was like trying to grasp water flowing through her hands.

She tasted of honey and spice, sweetness and surprise. She was addictive, Dylan thought. Over and over, the two of them had come together and he'd felt the strength of her. Now, he felt the give.

And found himself wanting to give even more.

He pressed his lips against her throat, inhaling her scent as she tilted her head back. He enjoyed having her just a little bit off balance, hearing the soft intake of her breath, feeling her shift just a bit closer to him.

And the need to give became a need to take. She was a woman accustomed to being in control.

He wanted to show her what it was like to lose it. He changed the angle of the kiss, tightened his arms.

As though the ground had abruptly shifted underfoot, Max found herself clutching at his shoulders searching for an equilibrium that she'd suddenly lost. Now, that furious need whipped through her, now desire didn't tug but raked, dragging out a response whether she wanted it or not.

She'd known what to expect, she'd thought. She'd gone in with her eyes open. A simple kiss shouldn't have taken her over.

It did.

He did.

If she were the curved steel, Dylan was the wave, insistent and powerful. A wave started from calm waters, rising and gathering, turning into an irresistible force. And like a wave, Dylan swept her up in a tide of arousal, carrying her along, whirling her around until he was all she could think of, all she could feel.

Dylan had known what to expect, he'd thought. He'd been wrong. It was like lighting a candle wick and discovering it was the fuse that started a bonfire. Max was ardent, greedy against him, her demand intoxicating. She stunned, she dazzled. And yet as much as she took, she gave far more, meeting him passion for passion, throwing all of herself into the embrace. It was too much and yet so far from enough. He burned with the need to have her. Not just her body, her, all of her.

It was that thought that had him breaking the kiss, raising his head to look down at her even as desire surged through his veins.

Max watched him, waiting for the beat of her heart to slow.

Not entirely sure that it ever would.

What she'd just experienced hadn't had anything to do with surprise or anger. She couldn't blame it on being dragged into it. He'd given her the choice, and she had made one. It hadn't been about the heat of the moment. It had been about desire, pure and simple.

But there was nothing simple about deciding what happened next.

Dylan stared at her, his gaze searching. He no longer looked like he knew a secret but as if he was looking for an answer. "If you start in with the 'I'm not interested in colleagues' speech, I won't be responsible for how I'll react."

"I wasn't planning to start in with that speech," Max said, stepping back. "Glory's going to be coming out in a minute. We should get back to the house."

"Don't hide behind that excuse."

"It's not an excuse. And I'm not hiding, I just have to think about this."

"You're right, we both do." He studied her. "And we both know what the answer's going to be."

Max shook her head. "I can't… I have to…" She turned for the house.

He caught her arm. "Why is this so difficult for you? What happened?"

"You don't—"

And then they heard Glory's voice calling from the house and Max felt a wave of relief. "Look, we should go in. You need to look at her sketches and decide what you want."

Dylan held her arm for just a moment longer before releasing her. "I know what I want," he said.

And she was pretty sure his words had nothing at all to do with art.

The cries of gulls, the lap of water against the pilings of the dock, the snap of sail in the breeze… they were the sounds Dylan had associated with summertime for as long as he could remember. He sat next to his father on the back deck of his parents' house, looking out at Casco Bay. The water glinted blue in the afternoon sun. A seagull landed on one of the dark pilings. A little way out from the shore, white sailboats bobbed at their moorings.

Hal Reynolds reached for his highball and took a sip. "You know, in all the years we've lived here, I've never gotten tired of this view. We may not have any man-made islands here shaped like palm trees, but you're never going to see anything like this in Dubai."

"You're right," Dylan said, "but Dubai does have

its attractions." It was funny, usually about this time in a visit he'd start thinking about some of those attractions, about being on the move, being in a place where anything could happen. This time around, the restlessness hadn't hit. Maybe it was because he'd been occupied with the proposal work. Or maybe because he'd been occupied with a pair of golden eyes.

If he could have marked it down to pure attraction, he would have been more comfortable. Then again, he hadn't been comfortable once since meeting Max. If the events of the afternoon had shown him anything, it was that whatever lay between them went far beyond simple chemistry. The thought made him a little uneasy. Of course, he'd never been one to take the easy out.

And he sure as hell was not going to walk away from Max simply because he was worried about getting in a little too deep. He knew where his life was going, he always had, and nothing was going to change that.

Not even a woman like Max.

Behind him, the screen door opened and his mother stepped out. "You've got half an hour to relax and then one of you two manly types needs to start a fire and char some beast for dinner."

Arianne Reynolds had the black eyes and brown hair of her Greek heritage, the same coloring she'd passed along to her son. She stepped up behind her husband's chair and rested a hand on his shoulder. He covered her fingers with his. "Give me just a minute and I'll take care of it."

"You two talk for now."

Dylan's father swirled his drink a little. "Now that you've had some time to work with her, what do you think of Max?"

Dylan could think of a whole lot of answers to that question, almost none of which were suitable to share with his parents. Go with the obvious, he thought. It was also the safest. "She's talented."

"Yep."

"Quick."

"Definitely."

"Too smart for her own good."

His father chuckled. "You mean too smart for your own good. Is she giving you a run for your money?"

"She can be challenging."

His mother laughed. "Sometimes those are the best kind."

"I figure we're going to lose her one of these days, probably sooner rather than later," Hal said. "I'm kind of surprised that she hasn't gone somewhere else already. She's got talent for bigger things."

"Maybe she likes Portland," Dylan suggested.

His father shook his head. "She's got bigger ambitions than that."

Dylan considered the idea of Max working at one of the other big agencies in Manhattan and found he didn't much like it. It would squash her spontaneity and either kill her spirit or leave her so frustrated that she eventually walked away. "Not everybody is as fair as you are. Some of the big firms can be pretty tough on women."

"I think our Max can give as good as she gets," Hal said. "I'm not worried about her. If she goes somewhere else she'll land on her feet."

Dylan glanced at him. "If you know she's that far along, why didn't you go ahead and give her the project?"

"She probably could have done it, but it's a pretty important project. I didn't want to take the chance of losing. What do you think? Is she ready to take on the next one that comes up?"

"She's definitely got the talent. And she's pretty clear about what she thinks needs to happen."

His father looked amused. "You sound frustrated. Do you want people on your team who have ideas? Or have you surrounded yourself with a bunch of yes-men? You need to have someone question you, make you account for yourself. Otherwise you run the risk of having an exploding ego. I used to be at one of the big firms, I remember what it was like. Why do you think I left Manhattan?"

Dylan blinked. "I thought you left Manhattan because you and Mom wanted to have family nearby once I was born."

"That was certainly part of it, but it was also a way to escape all of the jackasses." He held up his glass and squinted into the liquor. "I got tired of dealing with it and your mother got tired of hearing me complain about it. I figured I couldn't do any worse than starting my own firm and getting out from under it all."

His wife leaned down to kiss him. "I'd say overall, it worked out pretty well."

"They don't have places like this in Manhattan. Or Dubai."

Dylan smiled. "Is this the part where you start harassing me about coming home?"

"It would be nice to know that you're closer than an eighteen-hour flight away," he said.

"The more you badger him, Hal, the more likely it is he's going to stay away for good," Arianne said.

"I'm just saying."

"I've got no plans of moving to Dubai for good, trust me," Dylan said. "Although it is an eye-opener. You guys really ought to come visit before I finish up."

"Who knows, maybe we will." Hal gave his wife a speculative look. "I think your mother might look pretty fetching in a burka. Maybe it'll make her a more obedient wife."

Arianne punched his shoulder lightly. "Just for that, you're doing the dishes tonight."

"This is what happens when you get married," Hal said, shaking his head. "No respect."

Arianne leaned down to press a kiss on him. "But lots of love."

Chapter Eight

"Okay, now watch this." Eli Gardner, the stubby little BRS animation specialist, moved the mouse around as though he were playing one of the video games that occupied his every nonworking hour. First the Portland General logo, then the BRS logo floated up from the bottom of the screen to stay for a moment before dissolving into a view of the as-yet-unbuilt addition. In the background synthesizer music played with a pulse like the beat of the heart.

"Coming in from the parking lot with a pan shot lets them get the first impression," he said, narrating the action on screen. "Then we get to the good stuff when we hit the steps to the entrance plaza." The view rose abruptly to cross the brick apron, pan the fountain, then swoop through the sliding glass doors into the lobby to point toward the dome of the atrium.

Max reached for the back of Eli's chair. "Wow."

Eli grinned. "Cool, huh? Hal wants vertigo, I'll give him vertigo."

"Make sure you also give him the design," Dylan said.

"Have a little faith." On screen, the view rotated through three hundred and sixty degrees to show the lobby with its information desk and seating. Sunlight flooded the space. Little rainbow trapezoids thrown by a suncatcher dotted the floor. Then the viewpoint swung around the corner to where the long, unbroken space of the concourse opened out.

And she finally understood why he'd been so insistent on the changes. "You're right, the committee's going to love it," she told Dylan.

His look held both surprise and appreciation. "I'm glad you think so. It's too bad we had to make the trade-offs to get it."

"If anything's going to get us that contract, it's this," she said.

"Thanks." He held her gaze.

Her pulse bumped and just for a moment she could feel it all again, the pounding need, the furious desire, the almost overwhelming urge to cast aside all of her reservations and dive into the experience, an experience that might never come again.

"Guys," Eli said impatiently, scrubbing his fingers

through his curly black hair. "Okay, I'm going to restart it, so pay attention."

But it had been hard to pay attention to anything since that moment two days before. Oh, sure, Max had gone through the motions, she'd done her work. But through it all, her thoughts kept returning to what had happened between them, as though it were a puzzle she had to solve.

Because she did have to solve it. She needed to figure out what to do.

Trying to convince herself she wasn't attracted hadn't worked, and neither, it seemed, had trying to manage and compartmentalize those feelings. If the kiss at Glory's had shown her anything, it had shown her that the feelings were too big to walk away from.

And that she didn't want to.

But what she wanted and what was smart were two different things. Which brought her right back to the same point she'd reached over and over again in the past two days. She had to make a decision.

And, as she had over and over again in the past two days, she set it aside for later.

"—so that's what I've got so far," Eli said. "It's a pretty good, huh?"

"Oh, yeah, great, Eli," she said quickly. "Thanks for all the hard work."

"It's been fun. The guys in my gaming group aren't so happy about it, but they'll live."

Dylan glanced at his watch. "It's almost two. Why

don't you call it a day? It's Saturday, it's a holiday weekend. You've already put in enough hours."

"Cool." As though he'd just been waiting for the words, Eli started shutting down his software immediately. "If you thought I'd be one of those guys who'd say no, everyone else is working hard, too, you thought wrong." He picked up a videogame that sat next to his computer. "My Xbox and I have a date with Grant's copy of 'Fallout.'"

Dylan shook his head as they walked toward Max's office. "He makes me feel old."

"Of course he does, he's twenty-four. Anyway, you could have a date with 'Fallout' if you wanted, you just have to stop at an electronics store on the way home."

Dylan reached out and toyed with her earring. "I'd rather have a date with you."

Max stepped back quickly as Eli rose and turned toward them.

"I'll see you guys. Have a good holiday." He waved and turned toward the elevators.

"That's right, tomorrow's the holiday," Dylan said. "What time do you want me to pick you up?"

The clambake, of course. Max had hoped he'd forgetten. "You really don't have to go to that."

Out in the lobby, Eli's elevator arrived with a ping.

"Oh, I want to. Besides, I'd hate to disappoint your sister." He traced a fingertip down her throat.

"That was just Cady being Cady. She was just trying to tease me."

"Mmm." He ran his finger along Max's collarbone, sending little shivers through her. "I can see why she would. It's an appealing idea. I'll need directions to your house," he added, just about the time her legs began to weaken. "Just think, it's a chance for you to tell me what to do."

She swallowed. "Or where to go."

"No," he said. "I already know where we're going."

The thing to do was to be smart, Max decided as she gave her eyelashes a last brush of mascara the next day. Having an affair with Dylan—if she had an affair—wouldn't be the same thing as having an affair with a regular coworker. Yes, they were working together, but the situation was temporary. He wasn't actually an employee of BRS, and soon he'd be gone. Why shouldn't they pursue the attraction they both felt?

After all, she'd been attracted to men before and gotten involved with them. She had her share of affairs, even some very intense ones.

Never one like this.

The thought gave her a little stir of nerves. She could manage it, Max told herself. She only had another week with him. There was no way she could get in too deep.

The doorbell sounded as she was putting on her

earrings. Frowning, she walked to the door and opened it to see Dylan standing there. Something skittered around in her stomach. It was the first time she'd seen him in casual clothes. Not just casual clothes, but beach clothes that showed tanned arms and powerful legs. Somehow, it made him look even more male than before.

"Taxi," he said.

She blinked. "You're early."

"A bad habit, I'm afraid."

"I thought you were going to meet me downstairs."

"Change of plans," he said and waited. "Now is the part where you invite me in."

Max narrowed her eyes before moving back from the doorway. "Don't get any ideas."

She couldn't possibly have meant what she said, Dylan thought. A man couldn't look at her without getting ideas, especially not in that little white skirt that showed about a half a mile of legs. A red tank top and the blue earrings she was fastening on completed the ensemble.

"I'm a Yankee Doodle Dandy?"

Her smile came and went. Nervous, he thought. "I'm nothing if not festive," she said.

"You're festive and a whole lot of other things besides." It took an effort not to touch her. He figured he deserved some kind of an award for tearing his gaze away to at least make an attempt to look around her condo. The exposed brick walls of the living room went straight up to the second story. A staircase to one side let up to a second-floor loft that held her bedroom, he assumed. Which held her bed.

And that quickly, his mind was filled with the image of Max, naked, lying back on the sheets with her hair spread across the pillows as he moved to—

"—don't you?"

He'd tuned out, Dylan realized. "What?"

"I said, we could take back roads down but I think it would be smarter to stay on the main highway, don't you?"

A long, meandering drive with Max sprawled in the seat beside him certainly held its appeal, but they probably needed to arrive at the party at a reasonable hour. "Sure, whatever you think. Nice condo, by the way."

She sat on the sofa and leaned over to buckle on her sandals. A silver bracelet gleamed on a leather thong around her ankle. "I bought it right around the time this block was cleaning up. I got a reasonable deal on it. I'm actually close enough to walk to work when the weather's nice." She finished and stood up. "All set. Shall we go?"

"We could. Or we could just stay here and you could give me a tour."

"There's not very much to see," Max said as she grabbed her purse.

"Oh, I think there is."

At the look in his eyes, her pulse sped up. He

moved closer. Max raised her chin. "If you start with that stuff, we'll never get out of here."

"That's kind of the idea."

"What makes you think I've decided to sleep with you?" she challenged.

His slow smile sent something fluttering inside her. "We both know it's just a matter of time."

"Given that you're leaving in a couple of weeks, that doesn't exactly make it a foregone conclusion."

"All the more reason we should seize the moment." There it was again, that gaze that suggested he knew a secret, except this time Max knew exactly what that secret was.

And because she wanted to stay there with him, she forced herself to turn toward the door. "Are you going to drive us there, or do I have to?"

"My father warned me about demanding women." Dylan followed her out the door, shaking his head.

He'd swapped his usual luxury sedan for a sporty red convertible. With the top down and the wind in her hair on the open highway, it was impossible to be tense. Instead, she sat back and enjoyed the drive to Grace Harbor.

"I love hot days like this," Max said idly, moving one hand out into the slipstream of the car to surf up and down.

Dylan glanced over, amused. "Why don't you live somewhere farther south? Atlanta? Miami? Hell, even New York's warmer than up here."

"I've thought about it. I will when I'm ready."

"What are you waiting for?"

She watched her hand for a few seconds, banking it like an airplane. "I've been waiting to get enough experience, I guess. I don't want to go to some giant firm and just be a tiny little cog. I know how those companies can be."

"That's right, you interned at the Chicago Design Group."

She gave him a quick stare. "Have you been looking at my résumé?"

He shrugged. "It's part of the proposal package. I'm supposed to look at everything. I have to confess, I found it much more interesting than Eli's. But then I find pretty much everything about you more interesting than Eli."

"Gosh, well, count me flattered."

"It's not all just cog in the machine at firms like the Chicago Design Group, though. You can get a chance to see a lot of different kinds of projects. You can learn a lot."

Without thinking, Max snorted. "Oh, I learned, all right."

He gave her a quick look. "What happened?"

Her stomach tightened. "Nothing."

"You know, every time you start talking about how you don't want to get involved with a colleague, I get a really strong feeling that it's not just general caution. I get a feeling that something happened with you. Was it there? At Chicago Design?"

Max looked out at the highway unspooling before

them and let out a long breath. "Yes. I got involved with one of the architects when I was interning there. It didn't go well."

And he could feel her retreating from him. There was more there, but this wasn't the time, not when he couldn't touch her, not when he couldn't look into her eyes. So he set aside all those questions for later. "Why architecture?" he asked instead.

She relaxed a bit. "The standard answer is watching them put up an addition on our property when I was a kid. Before that, buildings had just been there, you know? All of a sudden I got to see the whole thing, start to finish. I got to see how the architects thought about the people and how they were going to use it. I figured, I liked art and I liked people, so it seemed like a good fit." She stretched out her legs and turned a bit toward him. "It was probably a no-brainer for you, being around it all the time. Did you ever feel pressured to be an architect?"

"No." In a gesture that seemed natural, he reached over to rest a hand on her knee. "I suppose if my dad were a different kind of man, maybe, but he never pushed me. In fact, it was almost the opposite. He encouraged me to try a lot of other different things. But architecture just felt right. I love the whole process of thinking about a problem and then, pow, the answer comes to you, like a muscle flexing."

"Do you have a lot of 'pows' in Dubai?"

Dylan snorted. "With my client? Constantly. He can be rather…challenging."

"The prince?"

Dylan nodded.

"How's my painting?" she asked.

"It misses you. Want to visit it?"

"I hardly think we want your father to know about this..." She waved her hand.

"This what?"

"Whatever's between us."

"So you agree that something is?"

Max looked down at his hand on her knee. "Yes."

"Have you decided what you're going to do about it?"

"I'm not sure."

"Let me know when you decide. Only, Max—"

"Yes?"

He stroked her leg. "Don't take too long."

The Compass Rose Inn looked as Dylan remembered, a sprawling, white clapboard house with a confusion of additions and outbuildings. Somehow, unlike Portland General, the effect was charming rather than discordant. Perhaps it was because of the rambling grounds and the plantings that softened the harsh edges. Perhaps it was the marina next door with its ranks of small sailboats bobbing at the docks. It felt welcoming and natural.

"Max! Dylan!" Cady waved and hurried over, tugging along a vaguely familiar-looking man in a white chef's coat. "You made it."

"All in one piece," he said.

"Meet my fiancé, Damon Hurst."

And the penny dropped. "Nice to meet you." Dylan shook hands with him. "I used to be a regular at Pommes de Terre," he added, referring to the chef's one-time Manhattan restaurant.

Hurst kissed Max's cheek in greeting. "Yeah, Pommes was great while it lasted. I've got a new gig here that's even better. You ought to come by sometime."

"That's right, I've heard about your deconstructed clam strips."

Hurst gave Cady a suspicious look. "What have you been telling people?"

"Just that you're the most fabulous chef in the world and I adore you," she said, leaning in to press a kiss on him.

"That works," he decided, pulling her close to kiss her longer and more thoroughly. "I hear you're doing some work in Dubai," he asked Dylan when he finished.

Dylan nodded. "The Al-Aswari complex."

"I'll be going over there soon. I'm working on a couple of restaurant concepts for Dimitri Stephanopolous."

Max blinked in surprise. "I thought you broke ties with him. Didn't you leave the Las Vegas project?"

"They came crawling after him on their hands and knees," Cady said with relish. "Now he goes out there a couple of days a month and consults by phone and Internet. He's going to take me to Dubai."

Max looked at her feisty, stubborn sister. "I'm not entirely sure Dubai is ready for you, Cady."

"Ready or not, here we come."

"Speaking of ready," Damon said, "we should go over and see how the pit masters are doing with our clambake."

The pit masters proved to be Max's father, Ian, and her cousin, Tucker. Tall, with thinning gray hair, Ian bent over the fire pit, working with Tucker to cover the smoking fire and hot rocks with alternating layers of clams and corn, lobster and potatoes, separated by seaweed.

"You two had better watch out for that smoke," said a pretty red-haired woman Max introduced as her mother. "You've been breathing an awful lot of it. We don't want you keeling over from fumes."

"We're fine," Tucker said, then ruining the effect by coughing.

"Humph. Come on, finish up. You've got enough food in there already to feed an army."

"All right, all right." With Dylan and Damon pitching in, Ian and Tucker draped a wet tarp over the fire pit and closed it off with rocks.

"Thanks," Ian said to Dylan. "Ian McBain, nice to meet you. I'd shake your hand but I'm not sure you want to smell like clams." He stood, taking a deep breath.

Amanda frowned at him. "Are you feeling okay? You look a little pale."

"I don't know, Tucker, I think next year I'm going to pass this off to you and Damon. I'm getting too old for this stuff. My arms are killing me from hauling rocks to the fire pit yesterday. Maybe I'll just take the rest of the day off and let all you guys do the work."

Cady snorted. "Yeah, like that's going to happen. Just for the record, Tucker and Damon were wrestling with him to lay the rocks in the pit. Someone's a little stubborn."

Ian reached out to tweak Cady's nose. "And from what I hear, I passed it on."

"I'll say," Dylan murmured, glancing at Max.

"What's this I hear about stubborn?" A tall man with Amanda McBain's smile walked up behind them.

"Walker, figures you'd show up after all the work is done," Max said, reaching in to give him a hug and a kiss on the cheek.

"It's no accident," he said as he circled the group, shaking hands and dispensing hugs. "I plan it that way. It's not easy, you know. It takes careful surveillance."

Max snorted. "Dylan, meet my brother, Walker, boy genius."

"I'm going to have to get myself a notepad," Dylan muttered.

"Nah," Cady said beside him. "Just say, 'Hey, McBain,' and you'll hedge your bets."

He nodded. "Thanks, I'll remember that." He reached over to tangle his fingers in Max's. "Hey, McBain, want to go get something to drink?"

It was an ideal party, relaxed, casual, with plenty to eat and drink. The sun shone and a breeze off the water kept things just cool enough. The crowd was a mix of family, friends, townspeople and guests, so that there were plenty of new stories to hear and old acquaintances to renew.

And there was Dylan.

He'd amused her, mesmerized her and aroused her. But as the day wore on and she saw him with her family, he did something she hadn't expected—he charmed her. He helped her father at the fire pit, he made her mother smile. He carried things out from the restaurant for Damon. He let Cady show off her greenhouse. And whenever Max caught his eye, he gave her one of those steady looks full of promise for her alone.

She was conscious of him everywhere she went, whether he stood beside her or not. She'd hear his laughter, glance up and catch him watching her. It made her very aware of herself and her body and its hungers.

In the fading light of day, she stood behind the gazebo on the little spit of land that pointed out toward the marina. Footsteps approached her from behind and she turned to see Walker.

"Hey, Max."

"Hey, Walker. Happy Fourth of July."

"Same to you. Having a good time?"

"Yeah, I am. How about you?"

"I guess. So, who's this Dylan guy? And don't try to tell me he's a coworker. I see how he looks at you."

Max laughed and turned to lean against the tree that grew in the middle of the grass. "Walker, are you suddenly turning into the protective older brother after all these years?"

"He's tougher than the ones you usually bring around." He watched Dylan help their father fold up the tarp from the fire pit. "You're going to have your hands full with him. I think it'll be good for you."

"What's that supposed to mean?" She pushed off from the tree and took a few steps toward the water.

Walker shrugged. "Usually you pick guys you can push around. I don't think this guy is going to push so easily."

"Thanks for the analysis of my love life," Max said tartly. "I was going to ask you how yours was going but I'm not sure I care now."

Walker moved his jaw. "Mine doesn't exist anymore."

Concern wiped away the anger instantly. "Are you and Elise still fighting?"

Walker shook his head. "No, the divorce lawyers have taken care of that for us."

Max stared. "You're getting divorced?"

"Got divorced," he corrected. "We signed the papers last week. Amazing how quickly you can push these things through if you've got enough money."

"Oh, Walker."

He put up his hand. "It's okay. It was the right thing to do. We've been separated for the last year anyway."

"But you never... Why didn't you tell us?"

"I kept hoping it would work out. And maybe I didn't want to admit that I was a failure. Anyway, the papers just put a rubber stamp on what we both knew."

"Is it what you want?"

He was quiet a moment. "Yeah, actually, it is. I mean, it sucks, but we weren't right together. I knew it the night before we got married but it was too late to call it off. Or at least I thought it was. I should've done it. It would've saved us both a whole lot of misery."

Water lapped against the rocks that protected the grounds. In the background, Hank Williams sang about being lonesome. Max put her hands on Walker's shoulders. "I'll spare you all the usual claptrap about new starts. I'm just going to say that you're somebody who's always had the greatest capacity for joy of anyone I know. It's been really hard to see you so unhappy. Now's your chance to get it all back."

"Is this the part where you tell me that there's someone out there for me?"

"Honey, there's someone out there for all of us."

He shook his head. "Maybe, but right now, being on my own sounds just fine. Thanks for the thought, though." He turned toward the food tables. "I'm going to go get a beer. You want to come with?"

"Nah. I think I'll just stay here for a while."

He mussed up her hair and turned to go.

There's someone out there for all of us.

Then she looked out across the party and her gaze met Dylan's. And the air backed up in her lungs. She'd tried to hold off. She'd tried to be smart, she'd tried to do everything she could to protect herself. But it was done, the moment of choice was long gone. Somewhere deep inside her, a thrum of awareness began. And like that moment of revelation he'd talked about on the way down, she knew.

She wanted him.

As though he'd somehow seen the message on her face, Dylan set down the drink he was holding and came toward her, gaze locked on hers, heat in his eyes. That humming connection sprang up instantly between them, practically visible in the fading light. Her heart thudded in her chest. She sucked in a breath that felt like pure oxygen.

He walked right up without stopping and fused his mouth to hers.

Time stretched out and became plastic. The only reality was the heat of his touch. Max broke away only because she had to breathe. "Take me home," she said huskily. "I want you."

The thirty-five miles to Portland passed in a sort of desperate blur. Max leaned over from her seat, nibbling kisses along Dylan's jaw, opening the top button of his shirt so that she could slip her hand inside. He tipped his head a bit toward hers, pressing his mouth to hers while keeping one eye on the road.

How had she managed to wait so long? How had she managed to fool herself into thinking that she wasn't desperate for this, desperate for him? Days had gone by while she'd delayed. Now, the passage of each second felt excruciating.

Just when she thought she could stand it no longer, Dylan pulled up before her building. He put the car in Park.

"God, I'm glad we—" Max began.

And he cut off the stream of words, dragging her to him for a voracious kiss that sent need sprinting through her. Max had thought of the devil the first time she'd seen Dylan Reynolds. Oh, but sin had never felt this good. It was like being on the Tilt-A-Whirl in the carnival, going around and around in every direction so fast that concepts like up and down and even reality had no meaning. She'd always loved those rides, not screaming but laughing at the sheer confusion of sensation.

It was nothing compared to what she felt now. His mouth overwhelmed, he ran his hands everywhere over her body, sliding his palms over her bare legs, making her moan. Making her ache.

Making her want.

Finally, he released her. "I've been waiting half an hour for that," he growled.

"Then let's not wait anymore."

But they stopped at the entrance to her building to kiss, and stopped again in the lobby. They lost long minutes outside her front door to the seduction of lip and tongue, the slip of hand. "We're wasting time," Dylan murmured against her skin.

"Are we?" Max dragged his shirt out of his waistband so that she could run her hands up his back.

They didn't bother with the ritual of a drink, they didn't bother stopping at the living room couch. They had only one objective, both of them, as they headed for the stairs.

There would be time to go slow, Dylan thought, but not when the need hammered at him, not when the hunger was this sharp. He pressed her against the wall at the base of the stairs, running his lips down her throat, sliding up that short, short skirt to feel her warm and soft underneath. Only when he felt his body tighten could he make himself release her.

Because he knew there was more.

Her bedroom took up the whole loft, an acre of soft carpet to cross before the bed—the bed—the place he ached to have them both. Impatient, he swung her up into his arms and strode across the room to lay her down on the duvet. She came up instantly onto her knees, reaching for him.

"I was thinking all night that you were a little overdressed," he said, running his hands down over her hips and then bringing them back up, sliding them under that stretchy tank top to find her curves. His reward was her gasp, as she threw her head back, giving him access to her throat.

Her scent filled his senses as he kissed his way across the fragile line of her collarbone and down toward the vee between her breasts. He stroked the satiny smooth skin of her waist, the sleek muscles of her back. It wasn't enough, though. He wasn't sure anything could be.

Impatiently, he brought his hands back down to gather the edge of her shirt and drag it off over her head. Underneath, he found warm bare skin and a lacy concoction that managed to look both innocently white and indecently transparent. It did nothing to satisfy the furious hunger that gnawed at him, just tantalized, tormented. He needed Max, all of her and nothing else.

Had she ever known this kind of furious demand? Max wondered desperately. Had she ever felt this kind of pounding need? He wasn't gentle and she didn't want him to be. She wanted to be ravished. She wanted to feel his hunger. His hands ran over her body, hard, almost punishing, and everywhere they touched she felt on fire. She ripped open his shirt, dragging it off his shoulders so that she could run her hands through the springy hair on his chest. When he peeled back the white lace cups of her bra, she caught a breath at the feel of the cool air against her and cried out as his hands slid up to cover her.

Then he was laying her down on the bed, leaning over her to drag off her skirt and the lace she wore beneath. He moved away long enough to strip off the rest of his clothing and then he was against her, on her, the feel of his bare skin against hers making her moan with pleasure.

He followed his hands with his mouth, running his tongue down over her chest, lingering on her breasts, tracing the flat of her belly.

His mouth was hot on her, pressing against the tender inside of her thigh. She felt the warm trail of his tongue on the soft skin. And then he found her, pressing his mouth on her, holding her down until her body bucked against him. And he drove her hard, dragging moans from her, making her quake with every slick caress until she tensed and tightened, shuddered. And then she was flinging her hands out to grip the sheets, her body arching off the mattress as the climax burst through her, one shock wave followed by another, and another.

Dylan moved up to lie next to her, taking her mouth as possessively as he had her core, feeling a sharp tug of arousal at the sporadic shudders that still ran through her body. "I've been waiting for that," he murmured against her lips.

Max brought a hand up to his shoulder to press

him flat on the mattress. "Not nearly as much as I have," she said, rising over him. "And not nearly as much as I've been waiting for this."

And she was avid and agile, moving against him, her hands not satisfying but tantalizing, making him want, making him ache for her in a way he'd never known.

She bent over him, dragging her hair over his torso, the silky strands slipping over the skin of his chest, his belly, and lower, until she bent down and tasted him, lingering there as he groaned, every atom of him focusing on her touch, that tease, that slick, hot caress. He groaned with her, tangling his hands in her hair, letting her take him closer and closer to the edge. Until he clutched her shoulders and dragged her up the bed. "No," he gasped.

"Now," she countered and moved up over his body to take him inside in a single swift motion that had him whipping his head back against the pillow. She bent over him, her hands on his shoulders, leaning down to press her mouth to his. He put his hands on her hips and she let him set the rhythm until he pulled her against him, turning them over as one so that she lay below him. And finally, as he'd wanted to for days upon days, he could feel her underneath him and bury himself in her.

And she was soft and strong and lithe, moving against him, driving him nearly over the edge with each tilt of her hips, each stroke of her hands. She made love with him the same way she lived, fearless, confident, throwing all of herself into it, matching him every step of the way. The same way she would always match him, he realized. But it was the look in her eyes, the naked need, that aroused him most of all.

He'd thought of a tornado the first time they kissed and now they rode the whirlwind together, the passion roaring through them.

Max laughed exultantly, raising her arms over her head and then draping them around his neck, sliding them down his back to feel the taut muscles flexing under her hands as she urged him on and on. She felt the tension gathering within her, winding tighter and tighter, filling her with an almost painful sensation. The surge of his body brought her to the line between pleasure and pain. Then the next motion flung her past it, pleasure exploding through her out to her fingertips even as he groaned and spilled himself.

Chapter Nine

The buzz of the alarm jolted Max awake to see the morning light streaming in through the skylights.

Monday morning, to be exact.

"Good Lord." She sat bolt upright, fueled by a jolt of adrenaline. Beside her, she heard a stream of curses from Dylan.

"What time is it?" he stopped long enough to ask.

"Six o'clock," she told him.

"And we've got the design review at eight." He was already out of bed, yanking on his shorts. "I've got time, barely."

"What are you going to tell your parents?" She crossed to the closet door to grab her robe.

"Probably nothing, why?"

"Aren't they going to wonder where you were all night?"

Dylan pulled on his shirt, searched for any remaining buttons and shrugged. "Maybe, I don't know. They were supposed to get in pretty late themselves. Besides, I've been an adult for a while now and they don't tend to worry too much."

He sensed rather than saw her stiffen. "Sure, because they're probably used to you staying out when you come to visit," she said, belting on her robe.

He took two quick steps and pulled her up against him. "No, as a matter of fact, they're not. This isn't my usual MO when I'm here. What's going on between the two of us is an exception…in a whole lot of ways."

He fused his lips to hers and the passing of time, so crucial just an instant before, suddenly became irrelevant. Long seconds passed, lost in the contact of mouth to mouth, hand to body.

Any reasonable person would've thought that the time they'd spent making love the night before would have slaked their desire, Max thought, but it had done nothing to dull the need. His clever mouth dazzled her, dizzied her until work became a distant, unimportant thought and the only thing that mattered was feeling his skin under her hands.

With effort, Max pulled away. "If you're going to get home, get cleaned up and back to the office in time for the meeting, you'd better go."

"I could take a shower here," he suggested.

Max's lips twitched. "Are you serious?"

"You're right." He started down the stairs. "I'll see you in the office in a little while." He stopped, then bounded back up the stairs for one last kiss, licking her lower lip as though savoring some decadent dessert. "That's got to last me all day," he said and turned for the door.

Max was sitting in the main conference room with the rest of the architectural staff, studying the plans and renderings taped along one wall, when Dylan came into the meeting just a moment or two after eight. Hal, she noticed, gave him a long glance. Dylan didn't look the least bit tired, not at all as though he'd spent most of the night before making love. She could still feel the ache between her thighs. Glancing down at her wrist, she saw a faint smudge of purple she knew had come from him.

And she felt the slow tightening in her belly.

Max took a deep breath. She'd known she was making a questionable decision in sleeping with Dylan in the first place. She hadn't considered what it would be like to sit across from him in a meeting when just two hours before, they'd been lying naked together in bed. That was the whole reason she'd avoided work involvements, the whole reason she'd tried to avoid this one, the whole reason she should stop it in its tracks.

Except that deep down, some part of her was

already calculating how soon she would be able to touch him again.

Hal stood with Leo Stein in front of the elevation view of the design Max and Dylan liked best. "This is the one they'll go with," Hal commented.

Next to him, Leo rubbed his chin. "It's a good design. All of them are. I'm just a little worried about whether we have enough wow factor. We're going to be presenting last, after the two hotshot firms. We need something that's going to grab the committee's attention."

Dylan stirred. "What about a model?"

"A model?" Hal frowned. "Nobody does models anymore."

"That's exactly why it'll work. Those other two groups are going to walk in with visualizations and animations like you wouldn't believe. After a while you lose the effect. No matter how good our animations are—and, Eli, they are really good—by the time we come in, everybody on that committee is bound to be a little burned out." He rose and began to pace as he talked. "People like having something to stand up and walk around and look at. Sure, it's old-school, but so are Fischer and Sherwin. They'll like it. No matter what we show them, I guarantee you they'll be staring at the model."

The room was quiet while everybody digested the idea. Leo was the first to break the silence. "It could work."

"Neither you nor I have time to do a model, Leo,"

Hal said in exasperation. "Outside the two of us, who here even knows how?"

Dylan turned to him. "I do."

"So do I," Max said. "I worked for an architect when I was in high school who was big on models."

"There. That's two of us," Dylan said. "If we can get someone to hit an art supply store, we can get started on it today. Assuming you don't mind working late, Max?"

She found herself fighting a grin. "Whatever it takes," she said.

How did he manage it? Max wondered afterward as she headed back to her office. Every time she got by herself, she began thinking how absolutely crazy she was to even consider getting involved with him, let alone diving into a full-blown affair. But then she'd see him. He'd flash that smile, look at her with those eyes and the next moment it all seemed like the most natural thing in the world.

Vulcans, she decided, had nothing on Dylan Reynolds.

Her phone was ringing as she walked through the door and she hurried over to pick it up. "This is Max."

"Is this Maxine McBain?" an unfamiliar voice asked.

"Max. What can I do for you?"

The person cleared her throat. "Uh, hi, Max. This

is Susan Harding from Portland General. I don't know if you remember me—"

"Of course I remember you," Max cut in. "The redhead, right?"

Harding laughed. "Yeah, people usually remember the hair."

"You're the oncology nurse." Max slid into her seat. "What can I do for you?"

"Do you remember how we talked at the committee meeting about what patients need and what that means for the design?"

Max wound the phone cord around her finger. "Absolutely. I thought you were dead-on then and I still do."

"Well, I wonder if it might help you guys to maybe talk to some patients about what they want before you design the addition. I mean right now, you're talking to us in the committee meeting but it seems like the focus of the discussion is about cost-cutting and things that work for the hospital. This would be a way to see the actual people." She paused. "What do you think?"

"I think it's a phenomenal idea," Max told her, staring at the floor plan displayed on her computer screen. "How do we get started?"

"After you left, I talked with Paul Fischer and the head of nursing. It took some convincing, but I've gotten the okay for you guys to come in and see what the patients have to say."

Max felt a little bubble of excitement rising in her chest. "Really?"

"I know it's late in the process, but it took me some time to pull it off. Could you and your partner come by tomorrow for an hour to talk with them? I realize it's short notice but this was the best that we could do."

"Absolutely, we'll be there," Max said. "It's exactly what we need. I can't thank you enough for thinking of us."

"If you give me those gardens or the family suites, that would be thanks enough," Harding said.

Max bit her lip. "I'll do my best," she promised as she hung up.

She rose and hurried down to Dylan's office. She could see him through the open door as she approached. He was staring down at plans on his worktable, eyes intent on the design. A sheaf of dark hair fell over his forehead. He wore an olive-colored linen shirt with the collar unbuttoned and the sleeves rolled up. It made his skin looked very dark. She remembered kissing his neck, pressing her lips to his shoulder. She remembered just how strong those hands of his were.

It was alarming how much of a fixture he'd become in her life in such a short time. She'd grown accustomed to his humor, to his smiles. She'd come to look forward to seeing him every day.

As though he'd heard her thoughts, Dylan glanced up to see her. The force of his gaze almost stopped her in her tracks. And she swallowed and walked forward to knock on his open door. "Got a minute?" she asked.

"Always," he said.

She stepped into the office, very conscious of his gaze on her. It was different, somehow, now that they'd slept together. Before, his gaze had made her aware of her movements. Now, it made her aware of herself, of exactly how responsive his touch could make her.

And exactly how much having an affair with him could interfere with her job, she reminded herself.

"Do you have an hour tomorrow afternoon to go over to Portland General?" she asked him. "I just got a very interesting call from one of the nurses."

Dylan wondered if she had any idea just how delicious she looked standing there in her slick little jacket and skirt, with those high heels that made her legs look like they went on forever. Of course, she also looked delicious in nothing at all and he was looking forward to seeing her that way as soon as possible. Making love with her the night before had been extraordinary; at least as pleasurable had been falling asleep with her in his arms.

He had a strong feeling that Max McBain was going to be a hard habit to break. Given that he was going to be leaving for Dubai in a week or two, that could prove a very big problem indeed. But there were things like telephones and airplanes. They could figure out a way to make it work if they wanted to, and he wanted to very much indeed.

"Come on in," he said. "Tell me about your call."

"You slept with him?" Glory asked Max.

They stood leaning on the fence around Glory's pasture, watching the photographer BRS had hired to photograph some of her sculptures.

"Can I tell you how not surprised I am to hear that?" Glory continued.

Max frowned at her. "You could at least pretend."

"Okay, give me a minute, here." Glory cleared her throat. "Wow," she burst out, "you really slept with him?"

"A little louder, please," Max hissed.

"I mean really," Glory said more moderately, "you think I should be even a little surprised after the way you guys were practically swallowing each other's faces when you were here last?"

"We were not."

Glory grinned. "Did you think it was just coincidence that you heard me making noise and coming out of the house after you broke apart? I timed it. I saw what was going on the minute you drove up. It was so obvious just watching you together what was going on."

It hadn't been to her, Max thought. Perhaps she'd

just been so busy trying to avoid the truth that she'd managed to miss it entirely.

"Let's see, he's gorgeous, talented, funny, successful—" Glory glanced over at Max "—am I missing anything? What's the problem with getting involved with him?"

"Glory, come on. I work for him. I just spent all of last night having sex with my boss."

Glory frowned. "Wait a minute. Dylan's running the proposal team now, right? Now, at the gala, you specifically told me Jeremy was not your boss, and Dylan took over for Jeremy, ergo, Dylan is not your boss," she finished triumphantly.

"I report to him on the project, I work with him." Max dragged her hands through her hair. "It's the same difference."

In the field, the photographer knelt in front of the wave sculpture to snap a shot.

"I still don't see the problem," Glory said. "I mean, so what, you're working together. It's completely short-term. He doesn't work for the company and he'll be gone before you can blink." She looked at the expression on Max's face. "Oops."

"No, it's true," Max said, willing herself to believe it. "I mean, that's the good thing about the situation, right? It can't go anywhere. I've got a built-in fail-safe." That was what she'd told herself before she'd gone to bed with him; why didn't it help now?

"It seems to me that as long as the two of you are

professionals, there shouldn't be any problem with the whole work thing." Glory climbed up to sit on the fence facing Max.

Max shook her head. "That's the problem. It doesn't matter how hard we work or whether being involved with each other affects anything. What matters is what people think." She stepped up to the fence to rest her arms on it. "Architecture is a really tough profession for women. It's hard to get ahead. The minute anyone in the office finds out I've been sleeping around—especially with the boss's son—my credibility goes straight out the window, along with any authority I have. Especially when I'm working under him—"

"So to speak." Glory grinned.

"That's exactly what I'm talking about," Max flared. "I don't want to turn into an office punch line." She knew how easily it could happen. She knew better and yet that hadn't stopped her. All it had taken was that persuasive mouth and those talented hands and she'd turned to mush. "I tell myself I'm too smart, I tell myself I know better than to do this and then…"

"What?"

She shook her head. "And then he looks at me and touches me and suddenly none of that matters anymore. And it scares the hell out of me."

"I think it sounds delish," Glory said.

"Wait until it happens to you."

Glory patted her shoulder. "I think you're getting spun up over nothing. I mean, you said yourself, he's going to be gone in what, a week? Two?"

Max shrugged. "I think it depends on when his client yanks his chain."

"Either way, the chances of anybody finding out in that span of time are minuscule. It's not like he's going to say anything. I don't think you have a problem."

Max's cell phone rang and she stared at it as though it were a scorpion. "Then what do I do?"

"It comes down to what you want out of it." Glory hopped down off the fence and stood next to her again. "You've got a gorgeous man who drives you wild in bed and is house trained. The way I see it, you've got three options. Option one, you can keep it going for the rest of the time he's here and store up enough orgasms for the rest of your life. Option two, you can keep it going for a couple of very busy days and cut it off, or option three, put the brakes on right now. You tell him it's over, you're done, that once was enough." Glory looked at her. "Was once enough?"

Max thought of the feel of his hands, the taste of his mouth, the way his eyes glinted with mischief when he smiled at her. And the bubble of joy she felt when they were finally together. She thought of it all before she slowly, unwillingly shook her head.

"No." She could feel the smile spread over her face. "Once is oh, so very far from enough."

"Ladies and gentlemen," Glory said. "I think we have a winner."

Chapter Ten

"I'm so glad you could make it." Susan Harding, the red-haired nurse, bustled up as Max and Dylan walked into the oncology department. "Like I said, we've got the go-ahead from the higher-ups, so as long as the patients agree to talk to you, you can just walk around the ward."

If he ever had to appoint a goodwill ambassador, he would choose Max, Dylan thought. She had a genuine skill. She didn't just walk up to people and start grilling them, she got to know them. It only took a smile, and she got them to relax and open up. Instead of asking questions, it became a matter of letting them talk.

"I've been in here for a week." Joanie Benjamin

rolled her eyes. "I am so starved to see something green and growing I can actually touch, I could scream. I mean, it's high summer. It's gorgeous out there but I'm stuck behind these walls. Even with the windows, I might as well be looking at a photograph or something on TV. I'd just like to get outside but..." She gestured to the tubes and machines connected to her. "Can you do anything for someone like me?"

Max glanced at Dylan. "I don't know. We'll do our best."

Joanie laughed. "That generally means no. After three years of this damn disease, I've gotten very good at detecting nonanswer answers."

"I'll tell you what," Max said. "Once we get the design and get it finalized, we'll get you an answer."

"Fair enough," she said.

They moved down the hall to the next patient and before Dylan knew it, the woman had opened up her wallet and was showing Max photos of her grandchildren.

"I had my surgery, and my kids were here around the clock," the woman said.

"What would you have different about the building if you could have anything, Florine?" Max asked.

"Besides a decent waiting room? Easy. A whole host of handsome young men like this one running around." Florine gave Dylan a lascivious wink.

The atmosphere at the center surprised Dylan. He'd expected it to be somber but, on the contrary, there was laughter, and a great deal of happiness. Perhaps the people who went there were extra-aware of the need to grab life with both hands.

The way Max was.

Dylan knew he was there to talk to the patients but over and over, he found himself watching Max instead. She moved around the ward, her eyes holding kindness, understanding, sympathy without pity.

They walked along some of the pediatric rooms. Max glanced into one open door and stopped. Inside, a little girl maybe seven years old sat on her bed, watching them with bright eyes. She held a coloring book.

Max knocked on the door. "May I come in?"

"Sure," the little girl said.

"What's your name?" Max asked.

The girl had a hot-pink scarf wound around her head. Underneath it, Dylan glimpsed the white of a bandage. "I'm Val," she said.

"Short for Valerie?"

"Short for Valentine," the little girl informed her.

"Well, I'm Max and this is Dylan."

Val giggled. "Max is a boy's name."

"My parents didn't like me very much," Max said in mock sorrow. "They must have known I was going to be trouble."

"You don't look like trouble," Val said.

"Looks can be deceiving," Dylan put in.

"I like your scarf, Val," Max said.

Val waggled her head. "I like yours, too. Max," she added and giggled again.

Max had wound a strip of gossamer blue and green silk around her throat that morning. Dylan remembered lying in bed, watching her dress.

"When's your birthday?"

"February 14," Val said. "My mom always says I was their Valentine's Day present."

"I bet that's why you're dressed like a valentine, huh?" Max slipped off her scarf.

"Yep."

"Well, February 14th is a long time away, isn't it? I always hated waiting for my birthdays, so I'm going to break the rules." Max leaned in next to the little girl. "You can't tell anyone, but I'm going to give you your birthday present today," she whispered, and wrapped the scarf around Val's neck. "What do you think?" she asked Dylan.

"I'd say you look pretty glam, kiddo."

Val's eyes squinched up and she giggled.

"Here." Max dug in her handbag and pulled out a little pocket mirror. "You can admire yourself. Now that's beauty."

Val posed in the mirror, for all the world like a fashion model. Then she handed it back. "Thanks," she said, stroking the scarf. "But I don't have anything to give to you."

"You don't need to give me anything," Max said.

"Yes, ma'am," Val argued indignantly. She looked around her bed table and then her eyes brightened. "Here, you can have this." It was a little angel with its skirt formed of a seashell. A tiny face had been glued on top, complete with a gold cord halo. Val pressed it into Max's hand. "You should put it up somewhere so it can watch over you," she said earnestly, "because everybody needs an angel on their shoulder. That's what my mom says."

"I guess your mom knows a thing or two," Max said lightly, but Dylan could hear the faint strains in her voice that matched the sudden tightness in his own throat.

"Picture time," someone sang out from the door, breaking the spell. They turned to see Susan Harding come in with a digital camera. "On my right, everybody lean in close together." Max put her arm around Val, and Dylan leaned in close to Max.

"Everybody say cheese."

The camera flashed and Harding came over to the bed. "Here we go, this is a nice shot. Look at you guys."

Dylan looked at the image on the camera display and blinked. It didn't look like people visiting a kid in the hospital. They looked like a family. Something twisted then in his chest, a tug that he'd never felt before.

Max walked over to Susan Harding before they left. "Can I have you e-mail me a copy of that picture we took with Val?" she asked, handing Susan a business card. "She's a great kid."

"Yeah, isn't she? She's doing really well. She's supposed to go home early next week."

"I can't thank you enough for setting this up."

"Did it help you?"

Harding had lovely eyes, Max noticed. "Yes, and we'll do our very best to get the patients what they need." She leaned in and gave the nurse a hug, then turned to Dylan. "We should go."

Outside, the air had turned a little cool. Max walked out the front steps but instead of heading toward the parking lot, she turned down the sidewalk, following it out to the end and staring toward the sea. Dylan came up behind her and rested a hand on her shoulder.

"You know sailors used to be able to see the hospital from the open sea," Max said quietly. "She was the tallest building in Portland. When they saw the spire, they knew they were home."

"Home is a good place to be."

"We have to do something for them." She turned and looked up at him.

"You already did something for them. You did something for Val."

"I didn't do anything."

"Sure you did. You made her smile. You're good with her. You were good with all of them."

Max moved her shoulders. "I can't do anything to help them. I felt like a fraud in there, listening to them, going through the motions when I know we're not going to use any of their input." She walked out on the grass, the wind blowing her hair around. "Remember Carl the janitor? He gave me the idea for the family suites. His grandson was very sick with spinal meningitis. They watched over him for days, camping out in the waiting room." She swallowed. "This is personal with me, Dylan. I want to help these people and I don't know how."

She stared into space for a moment, then shook her head. "Don't pay any attention to me. I'm just in a funk. Let's go."

"Where?" he asked.

She reached out to touch his cheek. "It's the end of the day. Let's go back to my place."

The afternoon shadows stretched across her bedroom as they stood beside the bed. Always before, they'd come together in fire and passion and impatience. This time the flash had turned into radiant heat that warmed without flaming. They'd seen much that day, joy and sadness. And somehow what they needed in this moment was to draw from each other, draw strength, affirm life.

He wanted to show her that she was treasured. He wanted to make her feel the tenderness he'd felt watching her that day. This time wouldn't be about speed and urgency. He wanted this time to be different. Unbuttoning her blouse, he drew it off her shoulders. Slowly, he ran his hands up the satiny smooth skin of her sides, feeling her tremble at the touch.

She was so sensitive, he thought as he finished undressing them both. He was so accustomed to the strong, confident woman that he had ignored this part of her. He laid her back on the cool sheets, then moved on the bed to lie beside her, pressing kisses on her forehead, her eyelids, trailing his fingertips over the length of her body.

He gave her sweetness, he gave her gentleness, as though she were fragile enough to break. Max was used to feeling female but rarely feminine. He brought that to her.

The heat built, but slowly. Instead of hunger, she felt longing. There was desire, but not as she'd known before. It wasn't a craving for physical pleasure, it was desire for this particular man, this particular moment.

Once, it had been a question of control, for her, for him. Now, control became irrelevant as they came together. In some way they became one, their bodies moving, flowing, the sensation that began in her body flowing into him. When they quickened, it was with grace and gentleness. And some part of her that was hers alone became his.

Dylan gave, and he discovered that in giving there was a greater arousal than in taking. When he heard that soft catch of her breath, when he felt the shiver run through her, it ran through him, too.

He moved up over her and slowly into her. And she

was beautiful, luminous, lovely in the fading light. And he felt that twist within him, that breathless moment when something let go inside. For just a moment, when they were joined, he stilled, staring down at her, his hands cradling her head, locked in this moment and its meaning. And then he began to move slowly, gently within her.

And she was around him, under him, within him. When he bent down to kiss her, open mouth to open mouth, they breathed one another's air. Together, their systems quickened. It was as though they were rising up as one, suspended by some emotion neither could name. He felt her tighten around him even as he felt need begin its slow build. And when they rose to a peak, they did it together.

He wanted to hold her, just hold her, Dylan thought, and absorb what had just happened. Because he knew right down to the fiber of his being that something essential had changed within him and that some part of him would now always be hers.

Max rolled over against him, draping her arm across his chest and resting her head on his shoulder. "'Night," she mumbled sleepily. He pressed his lips to her hair while her breathing deepened and she slid into sleep. For long moments he simply held her, listening to the sound of her breath, watching her face in the moonlight and thinking, wow; he thought about what to do next.

While he absorbed the fact that he was in love.

When she rolled over onto her back, he slid out of

bed and pulled on his trousers. Padding downstairs, he pulled a couple of sheets out of the printer in her office. And he sat down at the kitchen table and began to draw.

Chapter Eleven

The morning sun streamed through the windows as Max walked down the stairs, yawning. Dylan sat shirtless at her dining room table, a coffee mug by his hand. She paused a moment just to look. Seeing him in her house was still new to her, and strange. It felt good in a way that she wasn't at all comfortable with. She could get comfortable with this, Max thought suddenly.

Dylan turned around. "Did you sleep well?"

God, he was gorgeous, she thought. "Like the dead. You should have woken me when you got up."

"You looked like you needed to sleep. I kept myself busy."

She walked up behind him and put her hand on his shoulder. "What are you doing?" she asked.

A ruler and compass lay to one side, along with pens and pencils. Before him lay sheets of printer paper taped together and covered with confident pencil lines. And then she realized she was looking at drawings of the addition. Frowning, she pulled them toward herself and studied them for a moment—and then she realized what she was looking at.

"Oh, Dylan," she breathed.

Somehow, he'd done it. The drawings showed the lobby atrium and the concourse that ran along the addition. But through some magic, some flash of brilliance, some "pow," he'd figured out a way to bring back the family suites and the balcony gardens. He'd figured out a way to make it work. Something tightened in her chest.

"Like it?"

She bent over him and wrapped her arms around his neck. "Like it? I love it. You must have been up all night to do this," she said lightly, then took a closer look at his face. "My God, you really were, weren't you?"

He shrugged. "That's what coffee's for. Besides, I wanted to get the ideas down while they were fresh in my mind. There's a lot more work to do, and we don't have a lot of time to do it in," he warned her. "And Eli's going to have a fit because we're going to make him redo the animation."

"I don't care." Max bent down and fused her

mouth to his. The moment stretched out and she sank down into his lap, twining her arms around his neck, a bubble of something very like joy growing in her. Finally, with a sigh, she broke away, resting her forehead against his. "I don't want to say it—"

"Then don't." He took her mouth again with his, his hands warming her skin through the thin silk of her robe.

Gathering her resolve, Max broke away again, this time rising to her feet. "But we should really get over to the office if we're going to get this all done."

"After all that hard work and I don't even get a thank-you gesture?" Dylan asked aggrievedly.

"Well..." Max caught the sash of her belt in her hands and unfastened it. "Come on up to the shower and I'll see what I can do to demonstrate my appreciation." Turning toward the stairs, she let the robe slide off her shoulders and whisper down to pool around her feet. Dylan rose and she raced for the stairs, giggling, as he gave chase.

"I'm going to get you."

"Promises, promises," she said.

He'd been out of his mind, plain and simple, Dylan told himself as he sat at the computer the next night, rubbing his eyes. "Nobody in their right mind completely redesigns a project two days before the proposal deadline, you idiot," he muttered aloud.

That was what love did to a man, he thought, but he knew that wasn't it. No matter how much he cared for Max and wanted her happy, he would never have made the changes if the concept had been unsound. He'd redesigned the plans because she'd been right, because she'd understood what people needed, and that ability to understand—that caring—was one of the many things he loved about her.

The thought ambushed him, the same way it had all day. Dylan shook his head. It wasn't what he'd planned for his life, not yet and certainly not now. He hadn't expected to find himself in so deep. And yet in some ways, hadn't he? Hadn't he known almost from the beginning that things with her wouldn't be ordinary? Hadn't he realized that what was between them went beyond chemistry?

So he was in love; he'd spent the night thinking about it as he worked on the drawings. And over the hours, he'd come to accept it, even embrace it. The question was, what the hell was he to do about it?

Dylan crossed to his worktable where the model sat. He and Max had put together the main elements of the structure. What remained now was the time-consuming process of adding surface finish, detail work and landscaping. He picked up a plastic bag of little fake trees, weighing them in his hand.

Max walked in, lovely and golden, and he felt as though someone had just filled the room with oxygen. "Hey, you," he said.

She pinkened. "Hey."

"Eleven-thirty and still going strong. Who says we don't know how to have a good time." He grinned.

"Well, at this point we're the only ones who do. Eli and Grant headed out a little while ago. It looks like they're about done with the animations. Eli said he might do a little bit more on it at home."

"Does that mean I can kiss you?" Dylan asked.

She glanced out the door. "Only if you're quick."

He stepped in toward her, settling his hands on her hips. "Well, I don't know if I can guarantee quick." He nipped at her lower lip. "In fact, I'm pretty sure that I can't." He licked at her earlobe. "But if you want long and slow, I can definitely oblige you."

He pulled her to him and pressed his mouth on hers, taking his time, savoring her flavor, her softness, the curves he'd come to know, marveling at the fact that they somehow felt different now. Now that they were his.

"Not here," Max scolded.

"Why not? There's no one around. You said yourself, they're gone." He drew her over to his chair. "You can surely spare a little bit of time and affection for someone who slaved away last night...oh, and also redesigned the entire project."

Max laughed and let him pull him pull her onto his lap. "So you're telling me it's a labor to make love with me?"

"Oh, it is, but I'm a man who loves my work," he said. "And I'm dedicated to perfection."

There was magic in his mouth. For a few endless moments, Max let herself sink into the warmth of his kiss, feeling those lips trail over her cheek to her ear, where he started doing delicious things. Every part of her wanted to simply relax back and enjoy it, but she forced herself to break loose. "Much as I admire your dedication, we are still in the office." She resisted the urge to lean into him again and instead made herself rise and turn toward the door.

"Not so fast." Dylan caught her up against him and walked her backward toward the frosted glass wall. "I think we need to do something about this habit you have of always saying no," he said against her lips. "I thought I'd taken care of it already." He ran the tip of his tongue down her throat, pressing her arms up against the wall so that her bracelets clinked against the glass. "I guess I'm just going to have to see what I can do to convince you." He dropped his head down, licking his way over her collarbones and down to the tops of her breasts.

Max groaned. She needed to stop him, and she would in just another moment, but it felt so good and the tension was curling up deep in her belly and he was stroking her with his marvelous strong hands.

"If we were somewhere else, I know exactly what I'd do right now," he mused, "but since we're in the office, maybe I should just stop with this."

He ran his hand along her thigh, sliding it up under her skirt, trailing the tips of his fingers up to sensitive inner skin to find her where she was already slick and ready. "Did you say quick?" he murmured against her lips.

And he was touching her with his fingers, those wonderful, clever fingers, until she couldn't even think of stopping him, she could only move against him and concentrate on the feeling, stifling the urge to cry out. And the next moment, she was stiffening and gasping against him with the flood of pleasure, quaking until her leg muscles became liquid, able to stand only because Dylan held her up.

"Was that quick enough?" he asked. With a wink, he walked over to the worktable and begin putting trees onto the model. After a moment, on jelly legs, Max followed.

Making a model was exacting work, but somehow with Dylan it became fun. But then again, most things with Dylan were fun. She'd grown used to the teasing, the laughter, the sweetness. She hardly noticed the time passing until they were gluing on the last two trees.

"And that, ladies and gentlemen, is that," Dylan said.

Max glanced at her watch. "My God, it's nearly two in the morning. We're going to be wrecks tomorrow if we don't get to sleep. I'm going to—"

The ring of Dylan's cell phone interrupted her. He drew it from his pocket with a frown. "What the—" And then glanced at the display, annoyed. Letting out a breath, he answered the call. "Hello."

"Good afternoon, Dylan." The voice brayed out of the phone loud enough for Max to hear. "The prince sends his regards and his best wishes for your continued health."

"Please extend my best wishes to the prince," Dylan said. "Nabil, are you aware that it's two in the morning here?"

"But I see that you have answered the phone," Nabil responded.

"Only because I happen to be working late."

"If you were living here in Dubai where you belong, it would be two o'clock in the afternoon. You would be wide-awake."

At the mention of Dubai, Max felt herself tense. Dylan paced across the office. "But I'm not in Dubai," he pointed out.

Yet.

"You should be. And how is your unfinished business?" Nabil asked. "Is it now finished?"

"Not completely."

"You must finish it soon, my friend. The prince has completed his refinancing and the project is on a sound footing. We begin construction operations on Monday. The prince expects you back."

Her stomach twisted. Of course, it was time for him to go. She'd known it was coming, it wasn't like it was any sort of surprise.

What was a surprise was the way it felt.

"The prince will get me back when I am ready." There was an edge in Dylan's voice. "My business is not quite complete."

"If the business cannot be completed in the time

you have been there, perhaps you are better off abandoning it," Nabil said sharply.

"I'm not prepared to do that," Dylan said.

"Nevertheless, the prince expects you here in one week."

"What if I am not able to return?"

"Then the prince may find himself forced to make a change. If you wish to retain the project, I would advise you to do the prince's bidding."

"I don't respond well to threats, Nabil."

"What is the saying? It is not a threat, my friend, it is a promise."

Dylan stared at the phone in his hand. Nabil, apparently, had hung up.

A week. Max felt the words shiver through her. One week. Seven days and Dylan would be gone. And suddenly it was as though a chasm had opened within her.

She'd tried so hard to be careful, she'd tried so hard to be smart. She'd kept her distance, kept her guard up. The problem was that she'd kept it up so high that Dylan had sneaked right underneath.

And she'd fallen in love with him.

"Okay, it takes fifteen minutes to get to Portland General," Mindy said to the team at the end of the dry run the next day. "Allow ten minutes for traffic and five for parking and you need to leave here no later than ten-thirty. Dylan, Henry will have your car idling out front. Jason's got a van. He'll drive the model over separately and carry it in for you. I want you guys in the elevator and heading downstairs at ten-fifteen," she added briskly. "Any questions?"

The meeting adjourned. Max rose mechanically and left the conference room with the rest of them.

"You look like you could use some coffee, Max," Eli said, winking at her as he passed.

It would take more than coffee to fix what ailed her.

She'd known from the beginning that Dylan was going back, Max reminded herself. It wasn't as though it was news. On the contrary, she had depended on it. The time limitation had given her the confidence to take the involvement deeper, sure in the knowledge that he would be gone before she could really get in trouble.

Except that she'd been in trouble from the moment they'd met.

And now she—strong, independent, capable Max McBain—had to figure out how the hell she was going to live without him.

Dylan walked quickly by with the box of briefing books. "Meet you at the elevator in fifteen minutes," he said.

The ache she felt as he headed away was nearly physical. She gave her head a brisk shake. She couldn't do this, she couldn't let herself fall apart. The proposal presentation was an hour away. She had to focus. She couldn't let this consume her, not yet.

The thing to do was focus on what she had to do

next. If she did that, she could get through the next minute, and the next, and the next until he was gone. And then the days would pass without the reminder of his presence, and they'd turn into weeks, and the weeks would become months, and eventually it would stop hurting so damned much.

Resisting the urge to rub her chest, she headed toward the break room. She had to get some coffee or she wasn't going to make it. Maybe if she were more awake, it wouldn't all seem so impossible. Then, as she came around the corner, she heard voices. She froze. "Dude, I am not lying. I'm telling you, he had her up against the wall."

It was like having ice thrown down her back. Eli, Max thought numbly, it was Eli's voice.

"Man, it was late. It was just them. The only reason I was there was because I forgot one of my files."

There was a buzzing of a whisper that Max couldn't make out.

"Come on, I have my ways of getting into this place. No, I couldn't see exactly what they were doing but from the sound of things and the way she was moving up against the glass, they were having a pretty good time."

Horror filtered through her. They'd been seen. They'd been seen, not just together but…but…

It made sense now, the looks she'd been getting all morning. She'd assumed it was because she was tired but it hadn't been that at all. She knew, God, she knew, just how fast the office grapevine worked. And after a dozen years of being smart, she'd put herself at its mercy once again.

Of course, she'd had help.

She wanted to get miles away from Dylan. Miles away from any reminder of what had happened. Miles away from the person who had instigated it. It didn't matter that she'd been a willing participant. In that moment, she wanted to be as far away from him as possible.

"You've got to hand it to the guy, he's here for, what, less than three weeks and he makes off with the hottest merchandise in the store?" Eli's voice continued. "I'd like to know his secret."

There was probably more, but Max couldn't hear it through the roaring in her ears. Her stomach churned as she walked away. She wanted to drop to her knees. She wanted to throw something. She wanted to run as far and as fast as she could. Instead, she just felt vaguely nauseous.

How had she let it happen? How had she let it happen all over again? Some mistakes, apparently, were worth repeating or maybe it was just that she couldn't learn.

She took pride in never doing anything that would make her sorry. And suddenly, for the second time in her life, she had. Suddenly, her private life had become public fodder. Again. She was no longer Max McBain, architect, she was the hot babe who had done it in the office. Or who had been done.

How long before Hal heard? she wondered

miserably. How long before her status at the firm was compromised for good?

Or had it happened already?

She ducked into her office to get her things and headed for the lobby. Dylan walked up behind her, whistling. He took a closer look at her and frowned. "Are you okay? You look a little pale."

If she was pale, it was because of him. A surge of anger ran through her. This wasn't the place for the discussion they needed to have, but they needed to have a discussion, and soon. "Just lack of sleep," she said. "I'll be fine."

The waiting was endless, Max thought as she stood next to Dylan and Jason outside the hospital conference room. She paced, but not out of nerves over the presentation. She paced because it was the only way to keep from screaming.

"Don't worry, we'll be fine," Dylan said.

But they wouldn't be fine. As soon as she could manage it, there would be no "they" at all, and the sooner it was done, the better.

The doors opened and a quartet of men in suits filed out. The team from New York, she realized. An assistant beckoned to them. Dylan nodded to Jason. "Let's go."

Dylan pulled open the second door to the conference room and Jason walked in carrying the model. When he put it on the table, there was a little stir.

"Haven't seen one of these in a while," Fischer grinned. "It's kind of nice, though."

"The computer renderings never look like the real thing," Avery Sherwin agreed. "We spent all kinds of time going over computer models for our new headquarters and I was still surprised at the way it came out when it was actually built. This is better."

Dylan had been right, the model gave them their wow factor. The committee connected over it, walking around it, touching, talking about it. When Dylan finally stood up at the front of the room, looking heartbreakingly polished, he had their full attention.

"Good afternoon, and thank you for inviting BRS to submit a proposal on this project. As a local company, we think we have a unique perspective to offer on health care design in Portland. The proposal booklets contain full details on our team and our partners. But really, gentlemen, let's get to what's important here—a building that will serve your patient community in the most modern, effective and innovative way possible.

"Let me draw your attention to some of the unique features in the floor plan...."

She listened to him talk about the balcony gardens, the family suites, saw the committee nodding as he explained to them why it was the right approach. It had all been worth it, she thought. No matter the personal cost of working on the project, it had been worth it to have a chance to bring these innovations to the patients of Portland General.

If only their gain hadn't meant her loss.

"I thought that went well," Dylan said as the three of them walked out into the open air. Their one-hour presentation window had been stretched to nearly two, driven in part by an extended question and answer session.

"They asked to keep the model," Jason said. "I figure that's got to be a good sign."

"We'll know in a couple of weeks," Max said. You did your best and you waited to find out. It was kind of how life went.

Except sometimes you just got blown out of the water.

They crossed into the parking lot. "Okay, guys, this is where I peel off," said Jason. "I'll see you back at the office for the debriefing."

Max stayed quiet while they walked to the car and got inside. Dylan turned on the engine. "I'm glad that's over." He backed out of the parking spot.

"I can imagine." Her voice was cool. "You're done with the proposal and you can head on back to Dubai."

"This is about that phone call I got last night?"

"You mean the one with the prince yanking your chain?"

He moved his jaw. "Just because he's demanding that I be there doesn't mean that I jump."

"You were only here as an emergency fill-in," she said. "It's no secret that you have another life. There's no reason why you shouldn't go back to it."

"Just because I'm going back to Dubai doesn't mean that I leave everything here behind." He pulled out of the medical center grounds and onto the street. "What's going on with us isn't just a passing thing. I have no intention of letting it go. So if you're concerned because of what you heard on the phone call last night, don't be. You and I are going to keep going. No matter what it takes, we'll figure out a way."

"No, Dylan," she said tightly, "I don't think we will."

"What?" He stopped at the light and looked over at her. "What's going on, Max? You haven't looked right all day."

"Gosh, thank you very much."

"Tell me what happened."

"I'll tell you what happened," she snapped. "Guess what I heard this morning when I was going to get coffee? It was Eli, talking to a buddy. It seems he forgot one of the files he was supposed to take home last night so he came back and guess what he saw?"

"Oh hell."

"Yes, oh hell," she mimicked. "It was all over the office. I don't know how you missed it. I overheard people talking about at least twice more. Just like I told you at least twice more last night to please stop. But no, you were really in a mood. Even though we had so damn much work there was no way we were going to get it all done, you still had to take a break. You just wouldn't listen." Her voice rose.

"Look, I'm sorry it happened. I know it's embarrassing, but we'll live it down, we'll survive."

"*We'll* live it down?" she repeated. "Do you think you're the one they were making jokes about in the office today? Do you think you're the one they were staring at? I wondered why Eli was asking me if I was tired this morning and winking at me. And then I found out why."

"I'm sorry."

"Why are you sorry? You should be happy. Your rep has gone way up. The guys I overheard were very impressed that in less than three weeks you—"

"This isn't about the guys in the office," he interrupted, "this is about you and me."

"There is no you and me," she flared. "There never was. You were in town, we were working together, we fooled around a few times. Period. You go back to Dubai next week for your prince, so even if it wasn't already over it would be then. And trust me, buddy, it's over."

"Because I didn't stop?"

"Because you wouldn't listen when I asked."

"As I recall, you stopped asking pretty early on in the proceedings," he said.

She looked at him as though she'd been struck.

Dylan let out a breath. "Look, I didn't mean that to come out the way it did, but I still don't understand why you're so upset. It's going to blow over. It doesn't matter."

"It sure as hell matters to me," she shot back. "I don't get to escape to Dubai. I have to keep living with this, day after day." She shook her head blindly. "I can't believe I did this again. I cannot believe that I was so stupid."

He pulled the car over to the side of the road and turned to face her.

"Why are you stopping? We're two blocks away from the office."

"Because we are going to talk about this," he snapped. "What did he do to you? The guy in Chicago you told me about, there's more to the story. What happened?" She reached for the door handle and he caught her shoulders and held her in place. "You are not going to walk away from this, at least not without an explanation. You owe me that much."

"I don't owe you anything at all," she retorted.

"But you're dying to talk about it, aren't you? Go ahead, tell me. Tell me why you want to wipe me out right now."

Her throat tightened. "You want to know what happened? Fine. It began a few weeks after I started at the Chicago Design Group. Even though I was an intern, I had so much experience that within a couple of weeks, I was working with their entry-level architects. I figured that was why Elliott Seymour came by to talk to me."

"Elliott Seymour?"

"He was a partner."

Dylan let out a breath. "Yeah. I know him." The tone of his voice told her all she needed to know about his opinion of Seymour.

"He said he had a special side project that he wanted to work on with me in the evenings. I couldn't believe it. Here was this internationally known architect and he wanted to work with me. I thought that he was interested in my mind." She gave a bitter laugh. "God, I was more naive than I had any right to be. It started out with takeout at the office, then dinners. When he touched me at first, it almost seemed accidental. But it turned into more."

Of course it had, Dylan thought.

"He said he and his wife were separated, that they'd filed for divorce. When he took me to his condo, there wasn't a trace of her. And we slept together." She stared down at her hands. "It lasted for a couple of weeks. He kept telling me that I was special and that as soon as his divorce was final, we'd go public."

Max swallowed. "And then the company had their annual picnic. I don't know what I was expecting, it wasn't like he'd given me any reason to think he was going to announce us to anyone, but still…" She'd hoped. She'd bought a new dress she couldn't afford, spent hours getting ready. "I walked in and saw him standing there with this very beautiful, sophisticated woman. Who happened to be his wife."

"Oh, Christ," Dylan breathed.

"There wasn't any separation or pending divorce, just a wife staying with family in Europe for the summer. A wife and two sons. That was the worst part." She shook her head. "I felt dirty, just...sordid. I'd always sworn I would never have an affair with a married man. And here I'd done it."

"Not of your own choice," he said.

"It didn't matter. It happened." She let out a long breath. "The second worst part was the whispering. Someone had seen us one night, so they were all waiting for me to show up at the picnic, watching to see how I'd react. Especially the entry-level employees, who thought that Elliott was the reason I'd been on the fast track." She remembered the greasy nausea even now.

"I learned a lot about people that day, Dylan," she whispered, her voice barely audible. "All kinds of people. The liars, the users, the Teflon people and the ones who like to feed on other people's misery."

"They were watching?"

"Some of them were making bets," she said aridly. "Apparently this was a yearly habit for him. I'd won the intern sweepstakes for that summer but his wife had come home early. Most years, the interns never even knew."

She'd managed, just barely, to hold it together through the introductions, stood long enough to have a cocktail. And walked calmly and casually inside to the bathroom and threw up. She'd left as soon as she could manage.

"It all fell apart pretty quickly after that," she said. "His wife figured out what had gone on. I got called in to HR. Officially, they were downsizing me because of budget cuts but everyone knew the real story." And however irrational it was, she couldn't escape the fear it would happen again.

"It wasn't your fault."

"Of course it was. I thought I was way too smart to be taken in and I fell for one of the oldest lines in the book. So I figured I'd never let it happen again. Fool me once, shame on you, fool me twice, shame on me." She laughed bitterly. "It's shame on me, because I walked right into it again."

Dylan shook his head. "The hell you did. This is a totally different situation."

"Is it? I report to you on this job. Do you have any idea what people are going to think about me sleeping with the boss's son? Do you think anybody's going to believe I've earned the spot I'm in now?"

"Anybody who's been around this firm for five minutes knows you have. Max, I know this is hard, but it doesn't have to matter. It doesn't have to change things with us."

"Of course it does. It changes everything."

"Why?" he demanded. "I'm not that other guy. It's not the same situation. I'm not married, I'm not lying to you, I'm not using you. Dammit, I love you."

Panic sprinted through her. "Don't tell me that," she ordered, voice shaking. "I don't want to hear your lines."

"It's not a line." And he never would have thought it would hurt so much that she'd think so.

"I don't know why you care, anyway. You're going back to Dubai in a week. There's no reason to keep this going."

"I'd say there are a lot of reasons to keep it going," he said angrily. "We're good together, you and me, really good. But that doesn't matter to you, does it? You've been looking for an excuse to run from the beginning. This isn't about you and me, this is about Elliott Seymour." He held on to the steering wheel and stared out through the windshield.

"You've got a choice, Max," he said finally. "You can let it go. But you don't really want to hear that, do you? You'd rather keep doing the same thing you've always done, keep buffing up that pain. I always thought you had guts, but now I wonder if you really do. Maybe for the easy stuff, but when it comes to you, though, when it comes to really risking yourself, you're as big a coward as they come."

He turned the key in the ignition, but she already had the door of the car open. "Where are you going?" he demanded.

She was out before he'd finished saying the words. "Forget it, I'll walk from here." She had to be out of the close confines of the car, she had to be moving. If she could do that much, maybe she could stop thinking about everything she'd lost—the man she loved, her reputation, possibly even her job. A headache throbbed in her temples as she strode down the sidewalk. At the door to the BRS building, she hesitated, tempted, oh so tempted to keep moving. With every fiber of her being, she wanted to avoid going inside. She straightened her shoulders and strode forward.

Her cell phone rang, and she felt a clutch in her throat. Dylan. She was furious and frightened, but somewhere deep down, almost too far down to admit, she wanted him back. The phone rang again and she dragged it out. "Don't you ever—"

"Max." It was her mother's voice, but the tone sent chills down her spine.

"Mom, what's the matter?"

There was a silence. "Mom?" Max repeated.

"Max, come quickly. Your fa—your father's had a heart attack."

Chapter Twelve

The coronary care unit was dim and hushed. In this quiet place, no sense of the outside world intruded, only the beep and shush of the life-support machines. Privacy didn't exist for the critically ill—instead of separate rooms, the beds stood in open bays separated by dividers, allowing the staff to easily monitor and reach the patients. A brightly lit nurses' station occupied the center; around the periphery, all was dim.

Max followed the nurse to where her father lay unconscious, covered with a pale blue blanket. He looked gray and shrunken in some indefinable way. Fear choked her as she stopped beside his bed. Breathe, she ordered herself.

"Oh, Daddy. If you wanted attention, all you had to do was tell us." She gave an awkward laugh and reached for his hand. "You've got to get through this. We need you back. You're strong," she told him. But he looked so weak. She swallowed. "You've got to get through this for all of us. Most of all for Mom, because I don't think she can do without—"

Across the room, an alarm shattered the quiet. Bright lights flipped on all over the floor. Instantly, the staff sprang into action. "Code blue on 303," someone said urgently. Furious activity replaced the calm. Everyone there seemed to converge on the same bed all at once. "Defib, stat," a voice demanded. "Get me that adrenaline, *now.*"

Adrenaline sprinted through Max's veins. A nurse walked over to her swiftly. "We need you out of here, pronto."

Max headed toward the big double doors that led out to the real world. Behind her, she heard the thud and snap of the defibrillator. "We're losing him," someone said.

Then she was outside the doors and they were closing behind her, sealing out any further sounds.

But her heart still hammered, as though it were trying to do the work for the person who'd coded behind her. As though it were trying to do the work for her father. She hadn't told him she loved him, Max realized. There hadn't been time.

The families in the waiting room looked like refugees from some natural disaster, clustered together in anxious knots, hands clenched, faces pale. An almost palpable tension filled the air. Whoever had decorated the room had chosen subdued colors, probably intending them to be calming. Of course, anybody who thought colors could make a difference in a situation like this had never been through one.

Max crossed the room to her mother. Amanda McBain mustered up the ghost of a smile when her daughter sat down.

"How is he?"

Heartbreaking, Max thought. "Fine," she said. And compared to the patient in 303, he was fine. "They're going to be taking him into surgery."

Amanda's expression tightened. "They said they would."

"It's a good thing, Mom," Max said. "They'll fix whatever's wrong so he can recover."

Please, let him recover.

It was funny how everything suddenly got very simple in a situation like this. An hour before, her life had seemed unbearably complex. She'd felt buffeted by emotion at every turn: anger, sadness, loss, humiliation. Everything she'd tried to protect herself against for years had come to pass.

Now, none of those things mattered. They all seemed distant, receded into some distant, unreachable past. She couldn't even cry. Now, there was room for only one emotion—fear.

Max took her mother's hand. "Where's Cady?"

"Keeping an eye on the inn. We've got guests,

someone has to. Damon's out in Las Vegas this week."

How much harder it must have been to be Cady in that moment, unable to know exactly what was going on. And Walker down in New York, scrambling to get a flight up. It was going to take time for the family to get together, Max thought.

She only hoped they had enough.

"It looks like you and Max did the job," Hal said to Dylan as they walked out of the BRS conference room after the debriefing.

Dylan nodded. It was hard to remember that it mattered. He'd gone through the session on automatic, his mind returning over and over to Max and what had happened between them. She hadn't shown up in the office after they separated. It wasn't like her to walk out on work, but maybe she'd needed some time to get her emotions in order after their…what? Argument? Breakup? How could he tell his father the truth of why she had skipped the debriefing when he had no idea what the truth even was?

It was a hell of a thing, he thought later as he sat at his desk, waiting for the travel agent to find him a ticket to Dubai. He'd spent the better part of his adult life avoiding commitment. And now, when he'd finally found the woman he wanted to be with for good, she wanted nothing to do with him. It would have been almost funny if it hadn't been so pathetic.

And if he hadn't felt so damned empty.

He rose to walk past Max's office, glancing at his watch. Over three hours had gone by since she'd walked away from his car. It was hard not to wonder where she was. And yet the last thing he could do was call her. She'd made it very clear that was no longer his prerogative.

Dylan knocked on the open door of his father's office. "Any word from Max?"

Hal glanced up. "No. I've got to say, I'm starting to wonder. It's not like her to miss a meeting and it's definitely not like her to just disappear for half the day."

"Give her a call if you're worried," Dylan suggested.

Please.

"I probably will," Hal said, reaching for the phone.

Dylan made himself walk out of the office, even though everything in him screamed to stay, if only to hear her voice. But he'd heard her voice in the car. It still tore him, the things she'd said. Her hurts had been deep and lasting and it was naive to think they might suddenly evaporate, that like Glory's sculpture, the wall might transform to an open gate. Maybe at some point she'd get past it, but it wasn't likely to be soon. And it wasn't likely to be with him.

"Dylan."

He turned to see his father coming out of his

office, staring at him. Dylan felt the quick clutch of fear.

"What happened? Where is she?"

"Portland General." Hal paused. "Her father just had a massive heart attack."

Time passed differently in the hospital than it did in the outside world. In the waiting room, with its glare of fluorescent lights, the minutes crawled by while they wondered and waited. And yet there was no sense of time in this place where they couldn't see daylight, couldn't see the movement of the sun. It was like the outside world didn't exist. It was like they'd always been trapped in this place and this endless moment of uncertainty and fear.

Max tried without success to focus on a magazine. Across the room, a younger couple spoke in urgent tones too low to be overheard. By the door, a gray-haired volunteer in a blue vest sat at a desk with a green phone. Max glanced at the door for the third time in as many minutes, as though doing so would make the surgeon appear.

For hours now, her father had been in the operating room. For hours now, they had waited for word.

Next to her, Cady shifted restlessly. "Do you think we're ever going to hear from them?"

"Eventually."

"They could at least give us an update."

There was no point in being impatient with Cady when she was only voicing what they all thought.

"I imagine they have other things to do, Cades," Max said.

"It's not like I want them to stop. I'd just like one of the nurses to stick her head in the door and let us know how it's going."

"I'm sure it's going fine."

Unspoken was the worry that the reason they hadn't heard anything was because things weren't going fine at all. Max stared unseeingly at the magazine, resisting the urge to look again at her watch. Out of the corner of her eye, she saw a movement at the door. Her head snapped around.

And instead of a surgeon or a nurse, she saw Dylan.

She should have felt something, Max thought: anger, surprise, relief. But it was as though from the moment of her mother's phone call, she'd been enveloped in a hermetically sealed bubble where normal emotions couldn't penetrate. The events of earlier that day that had mattered so much now seemed like nothing, like they'd happened to another person in another life.

Maybe she should have felt something other than a sort of dull disappointment at Dylan's appearance but it wasn't possible when her ears were straining for the sound of the doctor's footsteps or the ring of the phone on the volunteer desk. It wasn't possible when she knew that a team of surgeons was fighting desperately to keep her father alive.

"Max." Dylan stood before her. "I'm sorry to hear about your father"

"Thank you."

He shifted. "What can I do?"

"I don't—"

The phone rang and they all stared at it. The volunteer answered it. She held her breath.

He glanced up. "Mr. and Mrs. LeFevre? You can go in now."

Disappointment flooded through Max as she watched them walk out. She stared at the door to the waiting room a moment, then looked up at Dylan. For an instant, some faint, dull echo of feeling penetrated the bubble, but then it was gone. "I don't... We're fine," she said. "But thank you for coming."

Thank you for coming. It was a sort of thing people said at funerals, Dylan thought. Her face was drawn with lines of worry, her gaze shell-shocked.

He hadn't shown up expecting anything. Certainly, he hadn't shown up expecting to continue their earlier conversation, or for her to fall into his arms. At this point, what was between the two of them had to be the last thing on her mind. The focus could only be on her father.

He probably should have stayed away. He'd tried to work for a while after his father had given him the news but it had been no good. Love didn't turn off and on like water out of a spigot, he was discovering. And maybe she didn't want him in her life, but just then if there was anything at all that he could do to make things easier for her he had to be there doing it.

No matter what she thought of him.

He checked his watch. Nearly five. "Have you guys eaten at all today?"

Max gave him an abstracted look. "I don't remember," she said vaguely. "It doesn't seem very important right now."

"If you want to be there for him, you have to eat. They have a cafeteria—"

She was shaking her head before he finished the words. "We can't leave. He's in surgery. They might come any minute."

"You don't have to leave. I'll go get it. You guys just tell me what you want."

"Anything," she said as her mobile phone rang. She answered swiftly. "Where are you?"

Dylan could hear the voice of the other person on the line but the words weren't clear.

"Okay," Max said. "Come when you can. We'll see you soon." She disconnected and turned to her mother. "That was Walker. He's on the plane at LaGuardia. He says he couldn't get a rental car but he'll take a cab out."

"Call back and tell him to forget the cab," Dylan cut in. "I'll go get him."

"Don't you have to be at work?" she asked, then noticed the time in bewilderment.

"The workday's over. Anyway, this is more important. You guys need someone to run around and do things while you're stuck here. You don't need to be worrying about getting Walker from the airport. I'll take care of it. Just let me know what you need done."

He saw the flicker of gratitude in her eyes and it was enough.

So as the hours passed and the day slipped into the evening, he chased down food, he brought coffee. He brought Max a change of clothes so she could get out of her suit and heels. The surgery went on, and they watched, and waited, and wondered.

Finally, Dr. Kiernan walked in. "Mrs. McBain?"

And every McBain in the room came to attention.

Amanda swallowed and stood.

"Your husband is out of surgery. The valve in his heart tore, which is why the repair took so long. We have him all patched up now. The next twenty-four hours will be most critical. If he makes it through that, he has a very good chance of surviving."

The doctor held up his hand before any of them could say anything. He looked exhausted, Dylan saw, with deep circles under his eyes. "Now, I want to be careful how I say this. When the valve tore, there was a lot of internal bleeding. When that happens, the body starts trying to compensate. He could be just fine, but you need to be aware that other damage could have taken place."

Amanda swallowed. "What does that mean?"

"Possible organ damage, for example to the

kidneys. There also could have been a period of oxygen deprivation." He hesitated. "He could have sustained some brain damage."

The skin on Amanda McBain's face turned dead white. But she squared her shoulders and her voice was steady when she spoke. "When will you know?"

"We're going to keep him in the medically induced coma for the next few days to help with his recovery. We'll start bringing him up out of it on Tuesday or Wednesday. At that point we'll see where we're at."

It was time to go, Dylan thought as he watched the surgeon walk away. This was a family matter. For a short while, he'd been able to help, but now Walker, Damon and Tucker were all there. Max had plenty of support. There was nothing for him to do. He couldn't intrude in this private time. So what if he needed to be there doing something for her? It wasn't about him. It was about what Max needed.

And right now she didn't need him.

He walked over to where she sat by her mother. "I'm sorry to interrupt. I just wanted to let you know that I'm going to leave you to your privacy and head out."

Amanda reached out to take his hand. "Dylan, thank you so much for everything you've done," she said, the strain evident in her voice. "We can't thank you enough."

"I can't say I was happy to do it because I wish I hadn't had to do it at all, but I'm glad I was able to help." He hesitated, looking down at Max, willing her to look up. "All right, I'm going to go."

She glanced at him with the same blank stare, her eyes smudged with exhaustion. "All right."

"Good." Walk out the door, he told himself. Just turn around and walk out the door. "Is there anything else I can do? Anything you need?"

"No." She looked at him but it was as though she was looking at some point miles beyond him. "Go ahead and go. I don't need anything from you at all."

So he left the hospital, and later Portland, landing in New York to return to a condo that felt no more personal than a hotel room. He went to his office and stared out the window, ducking calls from Nabil. He knew he ought to finish making his plans for Dubai but it was hard to be interested in it.

It was hard to be interested in much of anything at all.

As the days passed in the hospital, the McBains developed a schedule. The nurses only allowed two people into the CCU at a time, so they'd rotate which one of them got to partner with Amanda. Whoever had come out most recently did the food and drink run, though for Max, it was difficult to even think about food under the circumstances. It was difficult to think about anything.

Their access was limited, information even more

so. The nurses would promise an update in half an hour and four hours later there would be nothing. In desperation, Max took to keeping vigil in the hallway, sitting on a ledge that gave her a line of sight toward the entrance of the CCU. When the doors opened to let staff or visitors through, she'd get a glimpse of the unit. And her heart would hammer while she waited to discover whether the scene at her father's bedside was calm or a frantic stir of activity.

The only time she could really relax was at shift change, when the constant coming and going of nurses meant she got an extended view of what was going on.

She watched a pair of pretty young nurses pass by, one of them talking animatedly about her upcoming vacation to Cancún. It jarred Max for a moment. The real world existed outside the hospital walls. She felt as though she'd been living in this shadowy half world of fluorescent lights and tile floors for as long as she could remember.

There was an insistent and gnawing pain under her breastbone that she recognized vaguely as hunger. More from a desire to stop the irritation than from any real appetite, she slid down off the ledge and walked to the waiting room. She rummaged through a box of doughnuts that Damon had brought in and picked the least stale-looking one. Then she turned back to her post.

A nurse was just coming out of the double doors,

wiping her eyes. Something prickled on the back of Max's neck. She looked through the doorway.

And the rush of panic hit.

Seemingly the entire staff of the unit clustered around her father's bedside, some of them moving quickly, others just staring. And among them, just before the doors closed, Max saw the shining red of her mother's hair.

She knew the rules. She knew you had to wait to go in. She knew you needed permission. In that moment, it didn't matter. She slapped the square pressure switch that opened the doors and strode through, unable to stop herself, hurrying to her father's bed, the fear like a hand clutching her throat.

Only to see her father's eyes open and clear. He smiled up at his wife and held her hand to his cheek.

It robbed Max of breath. Any word she might have said died in her throat. For a moment she just stood there, swaying.

A nurse touched her shoulder. "I'm sorry, you're really not supposed to be—" She stopped when Max looked at her and just shook her head and handed her a tissue.

It wasn't until then that Max realized tears were streaming down her cheeks.

Dylan zipped up his garment bag and set it on the floor. Next stop, Dubai. Not that he was looking forward to dealing with the prince and Nabil again.

He wasn't looking forward to much of anything these days.

The week had gone by in a sort of stop-action frenzy. He'd sat in meeting after meeting with his staff, trying to compress weeks' worth of work into the few short days before he left again for Dubai. The problem was that his mind refused to focus on the work at hand for more than a few minutes at a time. Instead, it kept returning to Max, her father, her family. He couldn't help wondering how she was. The last time he'd seen her, in the waiting room, she'd been so far away from him he wasn't even sure she'd even registered who he was.

And every time he thought of her, he felt the punch of loss.

"Idiot," he muttered to himself. No matter what happened with her father, Max was done with him, she'd made that very clear. A smart man would take the hint and go on with his life.

So why couldn't he make himself do it?

Max stood outside the hospital doors, inhaling the fresh air, feeling the sun on her shoulders, really feeling it, for the first time in nearly a week. If she'd been sealed in a bubble for all that time, it had been taken away by the sight of her father conscious and alert, next to her mother.

Her parents' love for each other had formed the backdrop for her life. She couldn't imagine either one of them alone, she thought as she walked across the parking lot. The moment she'd seen her father press her mother's hand to his cheek had said it all, that one gesture encompassing a lifetime of love, the kind of emotion that built lives, the kind of emotion most people only dreamed of. The kind of emotion—

She stopped.

The kind of emotion she'd had with Dylan.

They'd kissed on the pavement where she stood, a kiss that had transported her, a kiss she'd tried to turn away from. As she'd turned away from him so many times, driven by fear. Like a wave, he'd kept coming back, wearing down her protests, showing her what could be between them. And coming back even after she'd told him it was over, coming back not because he wouldn't take no for an answer but because he wanted to help, asking nothing from her. Except that last moment she'd seen him, when she'd told him she needed nothing from him at all.

Her heart lurched in her chest. She'd been the worst kind of fool, lying to herself, lying to him, running from the best thing that had ever happened her.

Running from love.

And then she found herself running again, but this time toward something, toward her car, toward BRS—

Toward the most important person in her life.

"Max! How's your dad?" Brenda came around to the front of the receptionist's desk to hug her. "Everything okay?"

No, everything wasn't okay. Until she fixed things with Dylan, things weren't okay at all.

"My dad's doing much better, thanks. They say he's out of danger. They're going to release him to a rehab facility in a couple of days."

"That's great news," Brenda said, returning to her desk.

Max nodded, walking on into the main office, heading toward Dylan. Except she couldn't go more than a few steps without people stopping to ask about her father. She suppressed her impatience, answering the questions, trying not to wonder why he wasn't coming out of his office, too. A little stir of disquiet ran through her. Could the things she'd said to him have changed things irrevocably?

She swallowed. Maybe they had, but she'd never know until she talked to him. She had to take that chance.

Hal stepped out of his office and came over to give her a hug. "How's your father?" he asked.

"He's going to be all right," she said. "I'm sorry I had to miss so much work but I…"

"Don't think twice about it," Hal said. "Everything is here waiting for you when you're ready."

And because he was watching, she turned to her office instead of Dylan's, the place she most wanted to go. Maybe it was for the best if she took a few minutes to get herself settled and decide what to say. Then she'd ask him to go down with her for a cup of coffee and just tell him everything. Tell him she'd been wrong, tell him that she'd realized what mattered most.

Tell him that she loved him.

She walked through her door and stopped. A rectangular package wrapped in brown paper leaned against her desk. Taped to it was a note. Her heart began to said. She reached for the slip of paper.

For the memories. Dylan.

Fingers trembling a little, knowing already what was in it, Max lifted the package onto her desk and pulled away the brown wrapping.

And saw the sunset over Casco Bay.

Abruptly, she missed him so much it was a physical ache in her chest. She'd been such a fool. He'd been there and she'd sent him away. She had to find him now. She had to make this right.

He wasn't in his office and his computer was nowhere in sight. In fact, she saw with alarm, there was no sign of him at all.

She hurried to Hal's office. "Where's Dylan?" she asked, not bothering with the niceties.

"New York. He had some things to finish up there before he flies out to Dubai. Late tonight, I think," Hal said. "I can give you his office number if you need to talk to him about the project or anything."

"Forget it." Max was already turning away. "I'll find him."

The drive to New York was a blur. Still, it gave her something to concentrate on instead of waiting in the airport for hours to catch an afternoon flight and take the chance of arriving too late.

She hadn't, she thought, as she rode the elevator up to Dylan's offices. It was still early afternoon and if she knew him at all, he'd be at his desk finishing up. If she'd had more nerve, she would have called him on his cell phone, but this was a conversation they needed to have face-to-face. If nothing else, he deserved an in-person thank-you and apology.

And deep down, part of her was afraid that she'd discover she'd pushed him too far and lost him forever.

Dylan stared out the window, trying to get his thoughts focused. He'd spend a few weeks in Dubai, then look in on the Singapore project, and perhaps the one in Rio. Moving around would keep him busy, keep him distracted. Somehow, though, he couldn't face any of it with the same enthusiasm as he normally did. It wasn't because of the weeks in Portland, it was because of Max.

She'd talked once about home. It wasn't a place with your stuff, she'd said, it was a feeling, a person. And Max was his home.

He shook his head. "Dammit, no," he said aloud and rose. He wasn't going to walk away. Not like this, not without trying it again. He wasn't going to—

"Dylan?"

He froze, then turned from the window to see Max standing there.

She swallowed and looked to the side. "Um, do you have a minute?"

He nodded, not trusting himself to speak. She stepped inside and shut the door. She didn't sit, he noticed, but stood, twisting her hands together. She wore a pair of worn jeans and a T-shirt with a spot of coffee by the hem. Her hair looked disheveled and like it hadn't been washed for a few days. He'd never seen anyone look better in his life.

"How's your father?" he asked.

Her smile shone out, stopping his heart for just a moment. "He's going to be all right. No permanent damage. He came out of the coma this morning."

"That's great news. I'm really glad to hear it."

She took a deep breath. "I wanted to talk with you about what happened the day of the presentation. To apologize, for one. I said some things to you that I never should have said. I was upset, but still..."

"It was a bad situ—"

"No," she interrupted fiercely, "let me get this out. When we were in the car, you said something to me that I've been thinking about all the way from Portland. You told me that I was holding on to the past and that I was blaming you for what somebody else had done. You were right."

She bit her lip. "After everything that happened in Chicago, all I could think about was protecting myself so that it would never happen again. But it's like you said about Glory's sculpture, if you put up a high enough wall, nothing—and nobody—can get in."

He stepped toward her, heart thudding a little.

"What happened between us was the most incredible thing I've ever experienced. And I know I told you that it was over between us, but I was upset and I was scared and I was stupid and I was wrong." She looked at him, eyes swimming. "I was so wrong," she whispered. "And I don't know if I screwed up for good between us but I love you, and I don't want this to end."

He'd swept her into his arms almost before she stopped speaking. For a moment, he said nothing, just held her and absorbed the wonderful reality of having her in his arms again. "If you knew what the last week has been like," he murmured. "I thought it was over. The way you looked at me in the hospital the night I left—"

She stopped him with her fingers on his lips. "That didn't have anything to do with you. I was so overwhelmed I couldn't deal with anything. And you stayed there, and you did so much for us, you were so wonderful."

He pressed a kiss on her hair. "I couldn't stay away. I couldn't know what you were going through and not try to be there to do something, anything. What I said that day in the car was the truth, Max, I love you. I love you," he repeated, just to hear the sound of the words.

"And I love you," she said in wonder at how good

it felt. "I know you have to go tonight but we can talk, right? And maybe see each other when you get back and try to figure how to make this work?"

"I have a better idea. I say you come to Dubai with me."

"Dubai?" She leaned away from him. "In case you don't remember, I've got a job and a pretty important proposal in the works."

"I have another proposal to offer." Dylan looked down at her, mischief in his eyes. "How about if you take a different job? I happen to know of an opening in New York for the right architect."

"Really? That firm wouldn't be Reynolds Design International, would it?"

"No, I believe it's at a firm called Reynolds & Reynolds Design International."

She put her hands in his hair and pressed her mouth to his. "In that case, I'll take it."

* * * * *

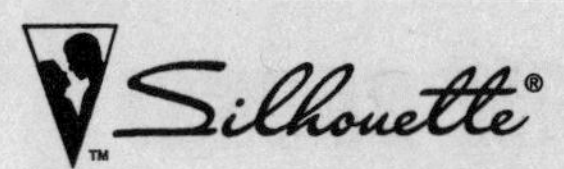

SPECIAL EDITION®

COMING NEXT MONTH

Available July 27, 2010

#2059 TAMING THE MONTANA MILLIONAIRE
Teresa Southwick
Montana Mavericks: Thunder Canyon Cowboys

#2060 FINDING HAPPILY-EVER-AFTER
Marie Ferrarella
Matchmaking Mamas

#2061 HIS, HERS AND...THEIRS?
Judy Duarte
Brighton Valley Medical Center

#2062 THE BACHELOR, THE BABY AND THE BEAUTY
Victoria Pade
Northbridge Nuptials

#2063 THE HEIRESS'S BABY
Lilian Darcy

#2064 COUNTDOWN TO THE PERFECT WEDDING
Teresa Hill

SSECNM0710

Five hunky Texas single fathers—five stories from Cathy Gillen Thacker's LONE STAR DADS *miniseries. Here's an excerpt from the latest, THE MOMMY PROPOSAL from Harlequin American Romance.*

"I hear you work miracles," Nate Hutchinson drawled. Brooke Mitchell had just stepped into his lavishly appointed office in downtown Fort Worth, Texas.

"Sometimes, I do." Brooke smiled and took the sexy financier's hand in hers, shook it briefly.

"Good." Nate looked her straight in the eye. "Because I'm in need of a home makeover—fast. The son of an old friend is coming to live with me."

She was still tingling from the feel of his warm palm. "Temporarily or permanently?"

"If all goes according to plan, I'll adopt Landry by summer's end."

Brooke had heard the founder of Nate Hutchinson Financial Services was eligible, wealthy and generous to a fault. She hadn't known he was in the market for a family, but she supposed she shouldn't be surprised. But Brooke had figured a man as successful and handsome as Nate would want one the old-fashioned way. *Not that this was any of her business...*

"So what's the child like?" she asked crisply, trying not to think how the marine-blue of Nate's dress shirt deepened the hue of his eyes.

"I don't know." Nate took a seat behind his massive antique mahogany desk. He relaxed against the smooth leather of the chair. "I've never met him."

"Yet you've invited this kid to live with you permanently?"

"It's complicated. But I'm sure it's going to be fine."

Obviously Nate Hutchinson knew as little about teenage

HAREXP0810

boys as he did about decorating. But that wasn't her problem. Finding a way to do the assignment without getting the least bit emotionally involved was.

Find out how a young boy brings Nate and Brooke together in THE MOMMY PROPOSAL, coming August 2010 from Harlequin American Romance.

HAREXP0810